The In

MW01120397

Joshua.

Matel

New Star
Rising

Thanks for the
Interview. Awesom sauce.

TRACY
COOPER-POSEY

STORIES RULE
EDMONTON · ALBERTA

This is an original publication of Tracy Cooper-Posey

This is a work of fiction. Names, characters, places and incidents either
are the product of the author's imagination or are used fictitiously,
and any resemblance to actual persons, living or dead, business estab-
lishments, events, or locales, is entirely coincidental. The publisher
does not have any control over and does not assume any responsibility
for third-party websites or their content.

Copyright © 2017 by Tracy Cooper-Posey
Text design by Tracy Cooper-Posey

Edited by Helen Woodall
http://helenwoodallfreelanceediting.blogspot.ca/

Cover design by Dar Albert
http://WickedSmartDesigns.com

All rights reserved
No part of this book may be reproduced, scanned, or distributed in
any printed or electronic form without permission. Please do not par-
ticipate in or encourage piracy of copyrighted materials in violation of
the author's rights. Purchase only authorized editions.

FIRST EDITION: March 2017

Cooper-Posey, Tracy
New Star Rising/Tracy Cooper-Posey — 1st Ed.

Science Fiction — Fiction

Praise for *New Star Rising*

Cooper-Posey is an awesome storyteller and I love how she develops her characters. You won't be disappointed if you're looking for a journey into a never-explored futuristic world before.

It is not a novel that can be skimmed through. Take your time and enjoy the new world that is presented to you.

This novel is fascinating for its rich and complex story line set on multiple planets/worlds.

What an amazing book from start to finish.

What is there not to like? I found myself digging into this book and disappointed at the end of it because I wanted more now rather than having to wait for the next book.

A complex story line that draws you in then keeps you engaged. Nothing formulaic.

Well thought out story. The science fiction components are consistent.

Science fiction with real science! LaGrange points – I am so giddy.

Tracy Cooper Poser never disappoints. She has a marvelous imagination and is able to give her stories and characters depth while developing a truly novel concept in her books.

Chapter One

Kachmarain City, Kachmar Sodality, The Karassian Homogeny.

They had survived ten days in the Homogeny, yet Sang still found it difficult to ignore the constant attacks upon their concentration. Screens were everywhere — disposables, transluscents, impermeables for wet conditions, building-sized, thumbnail-sized, embedded in windows, luggage, shopping bags, vehicles and clouds. The spoon they used to eat breakfast had a long, narrow screen running along the handle. The faucets in the ablutions areas featured rosette screens on the activation sensors. Each and every screen offered a different data stream, a unique offering designed to seduce and hold the viewer's attention.

The babble had been overwhelming, at first. After ten days it had evolved into merely distracting, which was why Sang failed to notice they were being observed, until the man made his move. By then it was too late to counter.

Sang held still, on alert. They put their spoon down. Regretfully, they would have to miss breakfast.

The eatery was busy, even this early. Many of the screens were displaying a show featuring a self-confessed biocomp called Chidi who mocked and disparaged the people he met. The Karassians seemed to enjoy the show, enough to train screens to focus on it. Sang did not understand how they could enjoy the derisive negativity. It made Sang uncomfortable.

Therefore, Sang did not watch the screens as so many in the eatery were. They pretended to watch, which allowed them to measure the man's progress toward the far corner where they were sitting. The man would have to move around six long tables, with every stool occupied by noisy Karassians.

The man did not look enhanced. He did not look Karassian, either. He did not have blond hair or the pure, rich brown eyes that Karassians valued. That made him an outsider, as was Sang. Yet he was not Eriuman, either.

Was this the one? Sang waited with tense readiness.

"Will you look at the pretty one, then?" The question came from behind Sang.

"We're going to sit down right next to *you*, sweet one." A different voice. This one, female. Sang was jostled from behind, forcing them to look away from the stranger and up at the pair addressing them.

"You don't look like a Karassian, sweet thing," the woman said. She was native Karassian, visibly enhanced. Her bare arms featured metal sinews that sat on top of her white skin. There were plug-ins at both wrists. She would be strong, then.

The male narrowed his standard brown eyes. He had no chin and a large mouth. "That's a thick lip you have there, little one."

The swollen lip and the bruise on Sang's cheek were courtesy of a scuffle two days ago, when Sang had explained physically why they did not appreciate a hand groping under their skirt when they were trying to board a carriage. Sang had assumed that the disfigurements would deflect interest. They had not.

"Move over, sweet thing," the woman said, bumping Sang's shoulder with her hip. Her metal enhanced hand gripped Sang's arm, tugging them sideways and almost off the stool.

The man was pulling a third stool over to the long bench.

Sang sighed. "I do not wish to keep your company," they said.

"We're *good* company," the woman replied. She put her hands around Sang's waist and lifted them, then pushed the stool aside with her foot. She placed Sang on the relocated stool, her hands lingering. "Heavy," she remarked. "You may be enhanced under that odd skin of yours?"

"I believe the lady said she did not want company." The third voice was that of the man who had been watching Sang.

Sang was surprised to feel a sensation of relief trickle through them.

"She's with you?" The woman was irked.

"Told you someone would have her," the man muttered.

Sang looked at the stranger. "I am not with them."

His nod was tiny. "She is with me. Move on."

The woman looked at her partner. "He doesn't look en-hanced." Her fingers curled inward, in preparation.

Sang braced for action. They were close enough to the woman, but they would have to turn to get a grip on her. It could be done, even against an enhanced.

The woman shot out her hand toward the stranger. It was very easy to pick her wrist up as she thrust it past Sang. Sang squeezed. Metal tendons bowed. The woman shrieked.

A few heads turned, though not as many as Sang would have expected.

The stranger who was not Karassian gripped Sang's upper arm, not hard, but firmly enough for Sang to know they would not be able to dislodge the grip without causing damage. "Let her go," the man said quietly. "You're drawing attention."

"We are not nearly remarkable enough to do that," Sang said with a confidence built over the last ten days. Only Karassians like Chidi, with their extremes of social behavior, held anyone's attention for long.

The man shook Sang. "Let go."

Sang let the woman go. She snatched her arm back and cradled the wrist. "Freak!" she hissed.

Sang smiled. "If you insist."

The Karassian man pulled the woman away.

Sang got to their feet and moved past the pair. The

stranger held on to Sang's arm as they threaded back through the tables. Outside, the sun was dazzling. Sang adjusted their vision.

The man hurried them through the early morning crowds. Karassians did not stay at home if they could find a reason not to. Even though the standard work day did not begin for a while yet, the footpaths were as busy as they would be for the rest of the day.

"Where are you going?" Sang asked the man.

"Somewhere private."

"There is such a place here?"

The man glanced at Sang over his shoulder. "I suggest you not speak again until we reach that place."

Sang remained silent. The man did not remove his hand. Sang didn't protest. It would ward off others, if Sang was seen to be under his control. It simplified things.

The private place was one Sang should have anticipated. The day pod was the third in a row of ten sitting on the edge of the footpath between pedestrians and the occasional ground car. A retreat pod was one place where privacy would be honored, especially if the two of them were seen entering. Karassians liked their pornography, yet they still preferred a closed door for their personal couplings.

The pod accepted the man's scan and opened. He pushed Sang inside and sealed it again.

Sang sat on the wide divan that was the only piece of furniture, while the man turned off all the screens except one.

He called up the pod controls.

The sounds of the high street muted. Then the walls turned transparent, allowing bright morning sunlight into the pod.

"It's one way only," the man said. "I need to see if anyone is taking an interest in us."

It was possible to make the walls transparent in both directions. The first time Sang had seen such an arrangement, they had halted, unable to look away from the pair frantically mating on the divan. Others had also stopped to watch the spectacle with mild interest, masking Sang's surprise.

"That is sensible," Sang said, of the man's setting of the walls.

The man sat on the edge of the divan, then swiveled, bringing one knee up onto the thin cushioning. The flowing robe he wore spread over the divan.

"You're an android," he said. "Passing as a woman, which means you're from Erium."

Sang remained silent. This man was not a Karassian. He was not Eriuman, either. There were still too many unknowns for Sang to speak freely.

"You referred to yourself as 'we'," the man pointed out. "You gave yourself away."

Sang was genuinely startled. "I did?" they said carefully. They had been diligent with their references since arriving.

"No one noticed, not with the woman caterwauling about her wrist." The man grinned.

Sang held still, waiting.

His smile faded. He tilted his head, his eyes narrowing. "You're bruised."

"I miscalculated," Sang admitted. "Our study of Karassia told us women were legal equals of men."

"Legally, they are." The man's tone was very dry.

"The objectification of women is of an extreme I had not anticipated," Sang added. They looked up and around the interior of the pod.

The man rolled his eyes, taking in the pod, too. "Why did you not pass as a man, then? It would have been easier."

"There are reasons why being seen as a woman would be useful." Sang shut up again. There was no need to reveal anything yet.

The man considered Sang. "Two outsiders in Karassia. I have not seen another for days. The last was a convict worker. I have to believe that you being here is not a coincidence." He studied Sang with eyes that were not Karassian brown, but a gray-blue that was flecked with brown, an odd, discordant coloring that marked him as a stranger, as did his black hair and the growth on his chin and cheeks.

"You are not Eriuman," Sang said.

"I am a free citizen." He frowned. "We could circle around each other for days, too cautious to break the silence. One of us needs to speak."

Sang didn't answer.

The man smiled. "You would not voluntarily enter the

Homogeny, given how they feel about androids. You were sent. I am hoping you were sent by the man I reached out to, three weeks ago."

Sang drew in a breath and let it out. "Who might that be?"

"Reynard Cardenas."

Sang let their shoulders sag, as if they had relaxed. "What might the message have been?"

"Still cautious. Very well. I told him I thought I might have found his daughter, Bellona."

"Bellona Cardenas has been dead for more than ten standard years," Sang said.

"She's here on Kachmar."

"A member of the Scordini clan here, among rabid Karassians?" Sang shook their head. "That is not possible. The enraged outcry would have been heard across the galaxy, all the way to Erium."

"Not if they don't know who she was."

"Her genetic markers alone would raise suspicions." Sang curled down their mouth. "Clearly, you have never met an Eriuman."

"I have met more than one," the man replied. "Many times. I realize now that is why the Cardenas sent you. You are different enough to pass as a stranger, not an enemy. As a woman, you can get closer to Bellona without raising suspicions."

"I was sent because my loss would be an acceptable one."

The man frowned. "Reynard Cardenas did not believe my message, then."

"He sent us," Sang pointed out. "Me," they corrected.

"Yet he does not hope."

"No."

The man shook his head. "I have a DNA match."

Sang considered it. "You have seen her." Only someone who had been physically present could have acquired viable DNA for matching. Sang curled their fingers in against the little spurt of excitement and reminded themselves that they held no more hope than Bellona's father did. This was a fool's mission, gladly accepted to serve the Cardenas family.

"I have seen her," the man confirmed.

"It is impossible. Here?"

"She does not look as you remember her. Karassians think her to be one of their own, a very sharp tool in their war chest."

Sang laughed. "Now we *know* you are lying. Bellona would never fight against Erium. If a member of the Scordinii chose to side with the Karassians, the Karassians would have trumpeted it with heralds. They would have trained every screen in the Homogeny to lengthy broadcasts about her deeds. She would be a *cause célèbre*, a crack in the Erium Republic's united front. The Karassians would remind its people of that at every turn."

"You are more right than you know," the man replied. "For that is *exactly* what the Karassians do with her. Only,

13

they do not parade her as a turned Eriuman, for she is not. She is one of their most prized warriors and Karassians everywhere cheer her exploits." The man delivered the rousing litany with a downturned mouth.

"If she is not Eriuman, then…?"

"Bellona Cardenas does not currently exist. The woman you once served is now called Xenia."

Sang shot to their feet. "The *app*?" They shivered and wrapped their arms around themselves.

"Application, appliance, I know not what the proper name for them is, but yes, that is she."

"Apps are androids," Sang replied as calmly as they could manage. "Programmed for destruction, enhanced beyond belief. They fight. When they are not fighting, they are corralled away from Karassians who prefer their intelligent assistants not compete with them for attention."

The man spread his hands in an open gesture. "I do not disagree with you on any of those points bar one. Apps are not androids. They're people, reprogrammed for Karassian use, their natural talents enhanced. When they are not slaving at Karassian orders, they are tucked away and kept harmless and helpless."

Sang rubbed their arms, even though they felt no cold. "If this is even possible, then knowledge of what the Karassians have done would emerge. Rumor, at least, would have trickled out. How could you, a stranger to this place as much as I, possibly know what the rest of the galaxy does not even suspect?"

The man shrugged. "I know, because I was one of them."

#

Ledan Resort, Ledania, Karassian Homogeny.

Xenia spotted Thecla on the other side of the lagoon and gladness touched her. She made her way around the still, green water to where Thecla was limping along in the soft sand, a medic next to her. Thecla was holding her human hand next to her body, as if it was injured.

"Thecla!" Xenia waved to catch her attention and hurried as fast as she could to where Thecla halted, waiting for her. She couldn't walk fast because her quads were sore from a training session. Her back ached, too. She couldn't quite remember the dance movement that might have strained her muscles so much, yet Dana, her coach, assured her that her rehearsal had been excellent and the soreness would soon pass.

Thecla smiled when Xenia got closer.

"You're hurt!" Xenia exclaimed.

"Just my other hand. And my ankle." Thecla held out her human hand to display healing burns. "I spilled lead on it."

Thecla was a sculptor, which was why she had the metal hand. Although Xenia had never seen any of her work, she suspected that Thecla was very good, as she lived here in Ledan. "Did you go away?" Xenia asked. "I didn't know you were gone." It was only now she realized that Thecla had not been around for a while.

That was often true of her other friends here in Ledan. Xenia frowned, staring at the sand. "There was someone else, too…they didn't come back yet."

"Thecla went on tour," the medic said jovially. "To show her work."

Thecla smiled.

"How wonderful!" Xenia exclaimed. "I'm so happy you're such a success, Thecla!"

"Do you two want to have lunch together?" the medic asked.

"Yes, please," Thecla said.

"Yes," Xenia said. She liked having lunch with friends. There were lots of friends…weren't there? Now she was thinking about it, she couldn't recall any of their names.

"Xenia."

She looked up at the medic, uneasy.

"Come and have lunch. Forget about the rest. Food, then a nap and everything will be good again."

Xenia smiled at him. "That sounds nice." She followed them across the sand to the dining hall where lunch would be waiting, wondering if she was hungry.

Chapter Two

Kachmarain City, Kachmar Sodality, The Karassian Homogeny.

The man glanced at the time and got to his feet. "What is your name?"

Sang hesitated.

"Or should I just call you Indigo?"

Clearly, he knew something of Eriuman ways.

Sang brushed the material of the skirt over their knees, straightening it.

"You can call me Khalil," the man added.

"One name only?" Sang asked cautiously, for that was a Karassian thing.

"Ready," he said. "Khalil Ready."

Reassured, Sang responded. "We are Sang Cardenas Scordini de Indigo."

"The Scordinii," Khalil Ready said. He studied the single screen with the pod settings. "You'd better stick to a gender, Sang. It might prove useful, after all."

"We are female for now. It is not a simple matter to switch."

"You might have breasts, but you're not thinking

'woman'," Ready replied. He glanced over his shoulder. "Trust me on that."

Sang shrugged. "I can remain indistinguishable while I must."

"Not with that hair and those freckles. Although, if you don't scream 'android', it will do." Ready unsealed the pod.

"Where are we going?"

"I have an apartment on the north side of the city, where we can talk without fear of being overheard. Now I know who you are, it's time to plan."

Sang merely waited.

"No arguments?" Ready asked curiously.

"That is not my function."

"You argued when that pair wanted to play with you," Ready pointed out.

"That was different. They were an obstruction."

"I'm not an obstruction, then?"

"You speak of plans. It is your intent to find Bellona and retrieve her, is it not?"

Khalil Ready narrowed his eyes, considering Sang. "Yes, it is," he said slowly, as if his thoughts were not entirely upon what he was saying.

"That is the task to which I was appointed, too. For as long as our tasks are aligned, you are not an obstruction." Sang nodded toward the door. "Shall we?"

#

Kachmarain City, Kachmar Sodality, The Karassian Homogeny.

A sense of direction was built into Sang's biological functions, so when Khalil Ready back-tracked and crossed their trail three times, they did not become confused. "We should head farther north if your apartment is indeed in the northern area of the city," Sang said as they climbed down from the sky train platform.

Ready glanced at Sang. "In time."

"Where is the apartment, really?"

Ready didn't respond.

"There is no one following us."

"There are screens everywhere," Ready reminded them.

"Making it impossible to avoid being tracked, in which case, why try and simply draw attention to ourselves? To anyone watching casually, we are returning to your apartment for more sex, having begun the dalliance in the pod."

"Your pair from breakfast were hovering outside the pod when we emerged. I'm being cautious."

"I saw them. They meant to harm me for hurting her wrist, only they withdrew because you were with me." Sang smiled. "They believe you to be the stronger one, despite the evidence from breakfast."

"It's a gender prejudice," Ready replied. "You're combat trained?" he added.

"I have…seen the training." For many nights, Sang had been ordered to act as sentry while Max and Bellona had trained in the secret garden.

Ready sighed. "It was too much to hope that he might send an army."

"You should be grateful the Cardenas sent anyone at all. Besides, I have my usefulness."

"You've survived Karassia as a woman who has no idea what she's doing. You clearly have skills, although they won't help where I'm going."

"Where *we* are going."

"Not without combat training, you're not."

Sang placed their hand against Ready's shoulder and shoved hard enough to make him stagger. When he whipped around with a curse, Sang slammed him up against the building they were walking past and pushed their forearm against his throat. When he protested, Sang pushed harder, until he gave a choking gurgle.

"I said I had seen the training," Sang said. "You, on the other hand, have had no combat training at all. You would be wise to accept what help I can provide."

Ready nodded, his head moving infinitesimally, blocked by Sang's arm.

Sang let him go. "There is no one following. The screens are unavoidable. You cannot disorient me, either. I suggest a direct route would be best."

Ready flexed and worked his shoulders, then massaged his throat. Silently, he began walking again.

#

"If you were part of this Appurtenance Services Inc. program," Sang said, as they dug up another spoonful of protein pudding, "and the program wiped your memories when they let you go, why can you remember anything at all? Why can't you remember where they are? And why not just kill you out of hand, once your usefulness was at an end?"

Khalil Ready did not seem to mind the questions. He dug into his own food with concentrated relish. Yet there was a furrow between his thick, dark brows. Then he pushed the bowl aside with a firm thrust. "I cannot remember what I have not first experienced. I was unconscious when they dumped me back on the streets of Kachmar."

"You do not know where she is, then?"

"Somewhere on this planet. I wasn't out long enough for an interstellar hop."

"How would you know that?"

Ready frowned again. "Do you want your mistress back or not?"

"Bellona was not my mistress," Sang said stiffly. "I am assigned to Maximilian Cardenas Scordini de Deluca."

"Then why are you here?"

"Because the head of the Cardenas family temporarily reassigned me."

"I mean, why aren't you looking after this Maximilian?"

"Servants are not required while one is on active duty."

Ready nodded. "He's in the Eriuman Navy. I should have made the assumption. The odds were good."

"Max would prefer I spend my efforts in search of his sister, anyway," Sang added.

"Bellona is his sister. The plot thickens." Ready reached up as the assembler pinged and pulled out a steaming mug. Sang could smell the caffeine from the other side of the table. Ready sipped and sighed.

"So why didn't they just kill you?" Sang demanded. "I would have."

"You're a cold-blooded Eriuman," Ready replied. "Karassians prefer to do their killing at a distance. That's why they use apps for their in-person combat work."

"Apps that are actually people," Sang amended.

"It helps to think of them as just apps," Ready replied.

"Helps what?"

"It keeps the nausea at bay and lets me think," Ready said flatly. "The people running the program thought wiping my memory would be sufficient. I was counting on that." He held up his left arm. "I have a memory tab implanted, along with an emergency recovery memory that forms in the absence of more than seventy percent of my memory proteins."

"It activates if your memory has been deleted?"

"Exactly. Then it restores my memory from the chip. I woke up two standard months ago, lying in the gutter on the Messe, with no idea who I was or where I was. A day later, I knew what had happened."

"You met Bellona while you were in the program and that is how you acquired her DNA."

"She is Xenia. That is all she remembers, in between assignments. The assignments are programmed in, too. They are set up to complete high risk assignments and if they are killed, the program moves on to the next app. If they return, the assignments are wiped to eliminate trauma and stress and the pleasant illusion of an idyllic life carries on uninterrupted, making them biddable and pliant. All memory of her real identity is suppressed."

"Not wiped?"

"They used to wipe original memories, only it sent apps into psychoses that were unsolvable. Now they suppress them, so the original personality is there as a base, but severely retarded. It doesn't occur to anyone in Ledan to question why they're there, or what they're doing there."

"Bellona has been missing for ten years. She has been in this program all that time?"

"I don't know. No one does." Ready scowled. "Maybe. Xenia is the darling of the Homogeny's military, sweeping in to save their asses when they need a hero. The stories have been around for a long time, so maybe she *has* been there all that time."

Sang shuddered. "Do you remember *your* assignments?"

"I didn't have assignments." Ready put his cup down. "I was recruited because I am good with computers. I spent my time in Ledan maintaining the memory programs and data storage."

Sang nodded. "That is how you know so much about the

program."

"They repressed all will power, all self-determination." Ready rolled his hands together as if he was washing them, or wiping them of something disgusting. "I did what they told me, while the tab recorded everything, so it is only in hindsight I understand what they were doing. It was all quite pleasant and stress free, while I lived through it."

"And you remember Bellona?"

"Xenia," Ready said firmly. "If you saw her as she is right now, you would not recognize her."

Sang put her spoon down. "We must fix that."

"Gender, Sang."

Sang rolled her eyes. "You and I must fix it," she repeated.

"That's better."

She shook her head. "Do you have any idea where on the planet this Ledania illusion is?"

"From my memories, no. I have been researching Appurtenance Services Inc."

"They are an interstellar corporation, with holdings and branches throughout the Homogeny."

"I can read their official file, too," Ready told her. "There are three hundred and forty-nine subsidiaries, but only thirty-six inside the Sodality."

"How many on this planet?"

"Thirty-one." Ready shrugged. "They started here."

"Which means they have become established, with deep

roots. You plan to find Ledan via their corporate structure?"

"I told you. I'm good with computers."

"So am I," Sang said. She smiled.

"The entire Karassian Homogeny is distracted right now," Ready added. "They just 'annexed' the Alkeides system." He nodded toward the small screen above the assembler. There was footage playing that showed some rugged-looking, quite normal free-space humans in utilitarian clothing, hugging tall blond, brown-eyed Karassians, their new overlords, their gratitude shining on their faces.

Sang swallowed.

"The party will last all week," Ready said. "It's a good time to go unnoticed."

"Give me a smart terminal," Sang said. "I bet I can find Ledan before you can."

#

Cardenas (Findlay IV), Findlay System – three standard weeks ago.

Reynard Scordino had no patience for being kept waiting. As head of the Cardenas family and one of the senior members of the Scordinii, there had been no pressure for him to learn that grace. For that reason and because Sang knew it would please him, they hurried across the homebase at the first summons.

The Cardenas was in the family room, standing close to the field wall, looking at the snow piling up less than a meter away, his expression the neutral one he favored for most occasions. Sang could not recall Reynard showing strong emotions of any sort, not in all the time they had known him.

Iulia Scordina, Reynard's wife, sat on the cushioned bench surrounding the bathing pool, her feet together, her hair piled up in elegant curls on the top of her head. Her bare arms gleamed in the dazzling light the room had been set to. She was the epitome of Eriuman womanhood. When she saw Sang, relief touched her face.

Troubled, Sang presented themselves to Reynard. "You asked to see us, sir?"

Reynard did not turn at once. He watched the blizzard rage while silence filled the family room, broken only by the soft lap of water in the pool. Someone had been bathing only recently. There was a faint scent in the air that made Sang think of the gardens in late summer, thick with blossoms and the chitter of insects. That made Sang think of Max, who liked the gardens.

"How is Maximilian doing?" Iulia asked softly.

"We regret we have no news beyond that which we gave you two days ago, ma'am. When the current campaign to win Kalay is completed, we may hear more."

Reynard snorted, turning away from the snow. "This scheme of his to launch little ships from cruisers will never work."

"It may," Iulia said gently. "The novelty alone will give the Navy a distinct advantage."

"Firepower and size has won worlds for generations,"

Reynard replied. "Opening up the guts of a ship weakens it. It makes the cruisers vulnerable."

Iulia looked down at her hands.

Sang waited patiently.

Reynard's jaw worked, drawing attention to the long scar down the side of his face. The original wound had just barely missed his eye. Reynard had refused to have the scar corrected.

"The family received a message three days ago, Sang," Reynard said. "I think it is nonsense. Perhaps it is a scheme to lure us."

Iulia sighed.

Reynard's gaze flickered toward her. "My wife believes the message to be authentic, though."

"The message, sir?"

"An anonymous communique. They, whoever they are—" and Reynard's disdain for the anonymity was clear in the curl of his lip, "—say they have located Bellona."

Iulia bit her lip, her eyes downcast.

"You intend to follow up on this message, sir?"

"I refuse to waste resources and time on a fool's errand," Reynard replied. "I want you to go and find out what you can."

"We, sir?"

"See if there is anything to this."

"Then you believe Bellona is alive, sir?"

"No." Reynard's gaze travelled once more toward Iulia.

"The idea is ridiculous. If she was alive, then she would have contacted us long ago. She would not have let us linger in uncertainty like this."

Sang understood that Reynard was not doing this to ease his own doubt, yet if Sang supported Reynard's belief it would upset Iulia. Carefully, they said, "We can ascertain if there are any facts to be found, sir. Only…we must point that out we are a generalist assistant. Would it not be advantageous to use a mind built to analyze minutia? We can recommend two family minds—"

Iulia lifted her chin, her eyes wide.

Reynard shook his head. "Out of the question. The analysts are already fully occupied with the war effort." His gaze took in Sang in one glance. "You would not fit in there, yet you do not look like an Eriuman, either."

Sang compared their oddly marked flesh to the deep olive typical of Eriumans, especially those of the primary clans. No, Sang did not look like one of them. "Where is 'there', sir?"

"Kachmar. The prime city there."

The heart of Karassian territory. "We are to infiltrate Kachmar?" Sang asked, astonished.

"I don't care what you do there," Reynard said.

"How do we get there?"

"You're a generalist. Figure out a way. I'll have a copy of the message sent to you." Reynard dismissed Sang with an impatient flick of his fingers.

Sang turned and left. To not obey the dismissal was unthinkable. As they passed Iulia, she looked up at Sang. Her smile was gracious. Her eyes, though, were a riot of conflicting emotions. Pain. Fear. *Hope*.

The hope stayed with Sang, long after Reynard's command that Sang figure things out for themselves had faded to a subconscious goad.

#

Kachmarain City, Kachmar Sodality, The Karassian Homogeny.

Sang recalled the perfumed peace of the family homebase on Cardenas and compared it to her current environment with fond sentimentality.

The tiny apartment was designed for just one occupant. It was bomb-proof, radiation proof and vacuum proof, which made it an unaesthetic square lump of shield walls from which utilitarian furniture could be extended as needed. There were no windows, the light was not full spectrum, nor directional and the air was not scrubbed.

After three days, the air was thick with biological traces that Sang had to force herself not to react to. Instead, she focused on the task of finding Bellona.

When one of them was not using the tiny bed, they both sat at the equally small table, mining data. Sang deep dived into public and semi-public corporate records, looking for patterns and holes that would show where Ledan was located.

Ready, on the other hand, had five screens formed, including one embedded on the table top, all of them running news feeds, most of them at full volume. After three days of listening to them while concentrating on her own text displays, Sang realized that Karassians liked to scream. It seemed to be a cultural norm to scream at anything, in order to display pleasure, pain, anger, shock, amazement, even awe. A birthday surprise was greeted with cries by the recipient. A popular public figure made an impromptu stop at a local eatery, while the diners all roared in surprise and delight. War reports were greeted with shouts of joy. The celebrations for the annexation of Alkeides were dizzying marathons of drinking, dancing and uproar—especially when a lens was spotted.

There were even more negative outcries. A tearful woman wailed to her friends and the lens, outlining how her former liaison had treated her. Her friends, several hundred of them in regimented rows who listened with upturned faces and wide eyes, greeted each failure the woman itemized with thunderous applause and calls.

A man, enhanced to the point where his mechanicals eliminated any human movement or grace, yelled insults at the lens in response to another Karassian's listing of the ten best restaurants in Karassia. The restaurant rater was, according to the biobot, a fool, a bigot, a liar with not a shred of Karassian blood in him, and a Standard, to boot. As only Karassians received standard gene manipulations before birth meant the restaurant critic *had* to have Karassian blood seemed to be lost under the sound and fury.

There was far more anger than there was joy. Jilted lovers, furious neighbors, rejected job applicants, failed business owners, the bankrupt, the homeless, the house-proud, the rich, the poor, everyone seemed to live their lives on screens, while everyone disparaged what they saw on the screens. Sang found it exhausting to listen to. After a while, she didn't hear the words anymore. She just heard noise.

Until a name made her lift her head from the lines of data, shock slithering through her. "What was that?" she demanded.

Khalil Ready looked at her through the center screen. "See for yourself." He flipped the screen around and backed up the feed.

"…Karassian hero Xenia once again saves the day! Fifteen of our bravest infantry plucked out of an Eriuman hellhole, with not a single soul lost! Mothers are reunited with sons and daughters, thanks to *Xenia*!"

The screen showed a large crowd gathered around a landing craft. A platform had been built in front of the airlock and half-a-dozen Karassians in the dark brown military uniforms were cheering and clapping as hard as the people watching them.

In the middle was a tall woman with ice blonde Karassian -perfect hair and brown eyes. She was not smiling.

It was Bellona.

Sang's heart gave a little jump. The smooth hair, the skin, the eyes were all wrong, but Khalil Ready had warned her of that. It was the uplift of the chin and the full lips that were Bellona's. The ratio of physical dimensions were hers.

One of the officers standing next to her nudged her in the side and murmured something. Xenia raised her arm in a victory salute. She didn't smile.

The crowd went wild.

Sang leaned forward, absorbing the details. Were those brows the same as Sang remembered them being? Was the height the same? Her physique? Had the Karassians changed those, too? How much of Bellona had they erased?

Was this even Bellona? A pair of lips, a stubborn tilt of the chin…these could belong to any mother's daughter…

"The DNA was a match," Khalil Ready said softly, as if he had plucked the doubt from Sang's mind.

"Why are you looking at this?" Sang demanded, pulling her gaze away from the screen.

"There will be clues in the footage, if you look past her to find them." He tapped at the screens and five more images of Xenia appeared, all of them from different occasions. "There is hours of this stuff, going back years."

"Then why haven't you been examining this footage all along?"

"Because I needed to calibrate first." Khalil dismissed the screens. "I needed a baseline. The most random element on Kachmar is the weather."

"They don't control the weather?" Sang asked, astonished.

"They don't have to. Kachmarain City is in the equatorial zone and the weather is relatively stable. Yet it can still provide surprises. Unscheduled rainfall, storms, cloudy days and so on. All of that is recorded in every image, in every archive. Then there are time zones and nightlines. Footage stored in local archives has local timestamps, so while it is midday here, it will be midnight on the other side of the globe."

"Comparison," Sang said softly. "Did it rain here, the day it rained in the image Xenia appears? Was it dark or light… hot or cold? Karassians spend all their time outside and there are lenses everywhere."

"It is a cult of reflections," Khalil said in agreement.

"Eriumans say Karassian is an empire of a billion leaders."

"And no followers." Khalil grimaced.

Sang pointed at the central screen. "This actually works?"

"I found you, didn't I?"

Sang shut down her screens. "I'll help you."

"Is that your way of saying my way is better?"

"I have my own conclusions already," Sang said stiffly. "I will see what results your method produces and compare them."

Khalil snorted. "You're as stubborn as my brother. He never could say he was wrong either."

Sang blinked. She had not thought of Khalil in relation to family and friends. He was an individual who represented aide in achieving her goal. "Your brother...is like you?"

"We're brothers." Khalil shrugged.

"I mean, is he here? On Kachmar?"

"If he was, he'd be dead. Benjamin is one of the Homogeny's most wanted."

"Then he can't help us," Sang muttered.

Khalil grimaced. "It must be nice, your black and white world. Enemy. Assistance. Period."

Sang saw once more Iulia's eyes, the hope in them. "It is a very simple thing I do, yes," she said placidly. "It is the execution that is complex." She tapped the table. "Files, please."

Chapter Three

The Bonaventura. Coria City-state, Free Space.

Captain Benjamin Arany winced as the bio-sealer worked to close the slash on his arm and glared at Kopitar. "Careful, Marcel."

Kopitar scowled back. "It wouldn't hurt so much if you'd let me deal with it when it was fresh."

"Too much to do," Arany said, returning his attention to the screen. He manipulated the controls with his free hand, backed up the data stream and ran it again, watching the river of tiny aircraft emerge from the guts of the big Eriuman cruiser, like a river of deadly gnats. "This new tactic of the Republic's is a killer."

"Demonstrably not," Kopitar replied. "You're still alive." He put the sealer down and prodded the seal with the tips of his fingers, testing the new flesh. The mental forefinger was cold against the skin, making Arany shiver.

"We're alive only by an atom or two," Arany said. He beckoned Natasa over.

She held out the pad. "Everyone accounted for except one."

"How many dead?" Arany asked.

"Twelve," she admitted, her narrow shoulders falling.

"Thirteen," Kopitar said, straightening up. "Shore died just before I came to find you. Sorry."

All three of them paused to absorb that loss, while the bridge around them hissed and steamed, venting plasma and more, as techs and engineers worked furiously to make basic repairs and get the ship moving again.

"Who's missing?" Arany asked, recalling Natasa's comment.

"Georgina."

Arany frowned. "*Georgina?* How could she be missing? She's not even front line. She *lives* in the galley!"

"I don't know, boss," Natasa said calmly. "I've gone through the ship's roster three times. I've checked every squeezable space on board."

"What about the crawl space under the engine housings?" Kopitar said, picking up the sealer. "Kids like to get under there and Georgie is little enough."

"*Including* the crawl spaces," Natasa finished. "She is not onboard."

"We need one of those remote tracking systems," Arany groused. "This sort of exercise is a waste of time."

"Granted," Natasa said. "When we have the spare credits I'll rush out and buy one. In the meantime, I count noses. Georgina is missing and I can't account for how she left the ship. We've been in vacuum since the Eriumans appeared and granted, it was a bit chaotic for a while, but none of the sensors record airlocks opening, which would be one way she could leave."

Arany followed what Natasa had not said well enough. "A ship attached to us during the fight?"

"Not that we noticed," Natasa said. "I would say, not at all. In order to do that and not have us spot them, the pilot would have to have super-human reactions to lock on and not nudge us while they're doing it. They'd have to hack into the computer core's vault to get at the airlock controls and wipe any trace of them entering and leaving."

"No one can hack a core vault, can they?" Kopiter asked curiously.

"No," Natasa said. "That's why I don't think it happened."

Arany found his attention drawn back to the still image on the little screen. The river of ships, each of them vulnerable to heavy armaments, yet nothing could wipe out that whole cloud—not even the city-killers the Karassians were developing.

"*Fleets* of ships…" Arany breathed, as ideas popped.

Natasa bent to look at the screen, then at him. "No. Stupid idea, boss."

"Why?" he demanded.

"For a start, freeships are called freeships for a reason. A trader from Cerce would rather spit on a Laurasian freighter. The Luathian twin cities haven't stopped fighting in over a century."

"There's a reason I left New Veles, too," Kopitar added.

Natasa pointed at him. "Exactly. The Cheng-Huang disembowel anyone from Veles, no questions asked. You seriously think any of them would cooperate with any of the others, even to fight the Republic or the Homogeny?"

"What about fighting both of them off?" Arany asked calmly.

"Both?" Natasa laughed.

"I'm serious," Arany said.

"Those Republic ships are coordinated. The pilots trained to work together," Kopitar pointed out. "I don't think any freeship captain has military training or knows how to take orders, which they would have to do, for something like this to work."

Arany dismissed the screen while the image lingered in his mind. "*Something* has to change," he said morosely. "We can't keep going on this way. We fight and fall back, fight and run away to watch from a distance as the Eriumans or the Karassians claim another city state. We're supposed to be *free*, damn it."

Natasa and Kopitar did not laugh. They lived with the harsh reality every day.

"Boss, even if you figured out a way to get everyone to agree to fight together, do you have any idea how many ships you'd need to make the Republic sit up and take notice?"

"A lot," Arany said in agreement.

"*Everyone*," Natasa said flatly. "Every ship capable of firing a weapon would have to join in. I'm talking about every known free state out there and there's a hell of a lot more we don't know about, too."

"Exactly," Arany said. "There are vast tracts of the galaxy that the Republic and the Homogeny have not yet taken for themselves. *That's* free space. You think anyone who lives here wouldn't want to hold the bullies off?"

"It's impossible," Kopiter added.

"No, it's a goal," Arany said softly.

#

Pushyani Wastelands, Pushyani, moon of Pushyan (Ovid II), Free Space.

Nearly a standard century ago, the Eriumans had flirted with folding space, racing to beat the Karassians and be the first and therefore the only patent holders of a workable bridge forge. It would have made the current null-space generators and lengthy interstellar journeys obsolete and given the Eriumans a genuine advantage in both war and economics.

The working bridge forge engine had been massive, taking up most of the surface of the Pushyani moon. It had perked up the economy of Pushyan for over five years, drawing on workers and resources, plus entertainment and distraction for the Eriumans working on the moon.

The first and only trial of the bridge forge had been a success for the better part of a second. The materials used to build the generators disintegrated as soon as the hole formed, collapsing the hole and destroying the moon, including everyone on it. The radiation the forge had spilled across the system killed everyone who could not leave Pushyan quickly enough.

It was the last time a free city state worked in cooperation with either the Republic or the Homogeny.

The Karassians had laughed themselves sick over the disaster as they quietly packed away their own bridge generator prototype.

Now, all that was left was the ruins of a small city on Pushyan and a growing asteroid belt around it, as what was left of the moon spread out in a long tail of rubble. The Pushyani Wastelands were a metaphor for shameful disasters and overreaching. No one went there voluntarily.

Which was why Ferid used the ruined city as a base. He was never disturbed there. The system sentries had long since shut down, their energy depleted. There were no lenses, which he had found took time to get used to. The silence was broken only by cold winds whistling through girders and ruins.

The girl proved troublesome for such a small, unenhanced human. She refused to talk despite Ferid's encouragement. He even pulled up a speech translator and installed it on his second server and spoke to her in her native language, the server molding his tone into soothing, relaxing cadences, yet still she refused to speak.

Using his full array of techniques upon her would quickly break down her fragile body, but Ferid was creative, which was why the Karassian military was paying him so well. He found a small room with four walls and a roof. He built a door over the opening, then took away her clothes and locked her in.

After three days he went back to see what progress had been made.

The stench was overpowering. At first he was alarmed, because the girl lay still among the excrement. He brought water and she showed signs of life, so he held it away from her, until finally, she agreed to talk.

The cold and the lack of water had taken away her voice. He gave her a pad and stylus. Her hand moved slowly, with long pauses while she figured out the coordination necessary for each word.

What do you want to know?

He had already learned a great deal from his foray into the *Bonaventura,* where he had found her, although he had not had time to download the datacore while he was rooting around in it, so he had taken her instead.

He began with simple questions. Ship's compliment. Crew structure. Nothing that could not be learned by observation and educated guesses. Nothing that alarmed her, that might trigger her resistance. As her answers came more swiftly, along with demands for water, Ferid slipped in one question among the innocuous ones.

Where is Arany's base?

She threw down the stylus and crossed her arms over her small breasts.

"I will find it," he assured her.

She shook her head.

"You will tell me."

She shattered the pad and drove one of the shards into her eye and beyond it, into the brain.

Ferid stood over the cooling body for a long while, enjoying his astonishment. She had surprised him. She was a small creature from a race of little people of no account to anyone but themselves, yet she had made a grand gesture, a heroic one.

This was the third time he had tried to coax Benjamin Arany's people into revealing where Arany and his ships could be found when they weren't out harassing Karassian deployments. The first two had been equally as determined not to give such a simple fact away.

For a small moment and in an abstract way, he appreciated their fierce loyalty and dedication to Arany. If all his people were of this caliber, tracking down the troublesome free-stater's base would not be as easy as Ferid had first assumed it would be.

What would a whole army of such people be able to achieve?

His computational array told him that this was the primary reason the Karassian military had given him the contract. They were proactively working to destroy Arany before he even thought of building such an army. That was why the free-stater was on their most-wanted list.

Ferid went back to his ship to meditate and compute his next step. He was proud of having reasoned out the Homogeny's motives. Their military would not have come up with this idea on their own. There were rumors that the largest portion of the overwhelming military budget was used to purchase Bureau advice and predictions.

The actual processes the Wyan Oushxiu Generation 98 used to arrive at their predictions was a closely guarded secret. Ferid had collected bytes of data about their operations for years. He suspected the Wyan Oushxiu Bureau used AIs in clusters to make intelligent neural nodes, with the nodes all linked, building into a gestalt that generated super intelligence. Predictive social analysis was their specialty. It would take a staggering amount of computing power to arrive at some of the startling—and correct—conclusions the Bureau offered their clients.

Yet he, Ferid, a simple biocomp, had reached the same conclusion.

He really was very good at his job.

#

Kachmarain City, Kachmar Sodality, The Karassian Homogeny.

When Khalil's best guess matched Sang's prediction, they

both agreed the probability was great enough to commit themselves to the next step.

Sang looked at the dot glowing on the overlay map. The small island was part of an archipelago that had been bought by a research corporation that, once the tiers of ownership were traced back, was ultimately owned by Appurtenance Services Inc., which in turn was a subsidiary of the commercial development arm of the Karassian military.

"There's only the two of us and you can't fight," she said. "The security surrounding the island will be immense."

"And unimaginative," Khalil said curtly, glowering at her assessment of his combat abilities. "They've been running this place for nearly seventy years. They're complacent. They've never once had someone come back to haunt them."

Sang frowned. Khalil used unique phrases sometimes.

"They know their memory wiping works," Khalil added. "Once they tossed me back on the street, they forgot about me." He tapped his forehead. "I have all the security codes here, still."

"They would have changed them."

"Why? They know memory deletion works. They know it in their bones because not one word of this place has ever been heard. Why bother changing codes for something that will never happen?"

"I would."

Khalil sighed. "No, you wouldn't. Not if you were human and complacent. Trust me on this."

Sang considered the request. "Very well, we will do it your way, but we will build redundancy strategies, too."

"Spoken like a good little computer."

"Now you're being insulting. I am a sentient, fully functional citizen of Erium."

"With no matronymic."

Sang glared at him.

That seemed to make Khalil happy.

Chapter Four

Ledan Resort, Kachmar Sodality, The Karassian Homogeny.

Xenia appreciated Dana's suggestion that she take a day off from her training to lie in the sun and relax. She really did feel tired. There was an ache in her back and her arms that nagged. Even her neck was stiff.

She found a lounger already on the sandy beach rimming the little cove and pulled it into the sun. She laid on it and closed her eyes.

"Xenia, wake up."

"I'm not asleep." She opened her eyes. There were two people standing next to her. A tall woman with short, copper-blonde hair and a wash of freckles over her cheeks and nose. A man… "Ari," Xenia said, delighted. "You've been gone for such a long time!"

Ari nodded. "I have." He glanced over his shoulder. "I have something to show you. Come with me." He held out his hand.

Xenia frowned. "Where did you go?"

"Hurry," the woman said, her voice low.

Ari leaned down and picked up Xenia's hand. "It won't take long. It's not far away. Come and see."

Xenia resisted his light and steady pull on her arm. "I really shouldn't. Dana says I have to rest."

"You can rest afterward," Ari told her. He hauled, forcing Xenia to swing her feet over the sides of the lounger and stand, instead of falling into the sand at his feet.

Ari smiled at her. She had always liked his eyes, she remembered now. They were a pale color and flecked. "Good," he told her, tugging her forward. "Now, just a little bit farther."

"Ready," the copper-headed woman said.

Ari looked past the woman. "Damn," he muttered.

"Pick her up if she won't go with you," the woman said. "We have about thirty seconds before they see us."

Xenia frowned. There was worry in their voices. She hadn't heard worry in anyone's voice or expression for a long time. She had almost forgotten what it was, until just now. She didn't like the way it made her feel. Her heart was thudding uneasily. "I don't want to go," she told the two of them.

Ari's smile was all wrong. "You really do need to see this. I promise, it won't hurt you."

Xenia hesitated. "This isn't right." She didn't know what was wrong, precisely, but her uneasiness was building.

The woman made a vexed sound and stepped up close.

"No, wait!" Ari said sharply, his voice still soft.

The woman raised her arm. Something slammed into the side of Xenia's neck, just under her ear, then blackness dropped over her.

#

Ledan Resort, Kachmar Sodality, The Karassian Homogeny.

Ready bent and let Bellona's unconscious body fold over his shoulder, then straightened again. He glared at Sang. "Now we have to carry her, just when we need to sprint."

"She wasn't going to cooperate," Sang pointed out, rubbing her elbow. The blow had worked far more effectively than she had thought it might when delivered by someone who had never performed the motion before. "The memory inhibitors must also limit free will. You heard her. She was doing what her coach told her to do. The Bellona I knew would have done the complete opposite." She glanced over her shoulder.

The towheaded guards in casual clothing were coming closer, a tight knot of three of them, chatting easily. They had nothing to fear from the inmates. They were relaxed.

Ready hurried across the sand, heading for the little service corridor that ran beside the holographic wall. Sang followed. Rocks and tropical trees were arranged in front of the entrance in a way to discourage anyone from finding the corridor. They clambered over the rocks, Ready breathing hard.

"Shall I take her?" Sang asked.

He didn't answer.

Sang glanced over her shoulder as they turned into the corridor. The guards had reached the path that surrounded that side of the artificial cove, still talking. They had not been seen, although that would not last for long. Inside this most secure of Karassian facilities, there would be lenses everywhere. The only reason no alarm had been raised so far was because they had moved around the enclosure as if they were residents. Neither of them carried any weapons that might alert observers or scanners.

Now they had taken Bellona, someone would react. How long before that happened depended upon how closely the feeds were being monitored. From the casual, lazy air of the three guards, Sang judged that minutes might yet pass before anyone noticed that one of their apps was missing.

The walls of the corridor were covered in the mossy growth that permeated the enclosure, encouraged by the humid air. The humidity was uncomfortable, for Sang was used to the dry heat of Erium. She pushed ahead of Ready and eased open the door into the greater compound and looked around.

Still no alarm.

"Too easy," she whispered.

"It is beyond their imaginations that someone might do what we are doing," Ready said. "Back to the skiff, as fast as we can."

The air outside the enclosure was cooler, yet still damp, for it had rained only a short while ago. Puddles still lingered on the compressed and fused earth surface of the working areas. There were administration buildings on the far side, closer to the real beach.

The skiff they had stolen from the marina in Kachmarain City lay keel-up on a stony shore on the other side of the island. It had taken them all night to navigate through the swampy interior. It would take them longer to return, but as long as they stayed lower than two meters above ground at all times, they would not register on the passive scans covering the island. The same lack of imagination had presumed that no one would attempt to approach the island other than by air and had set the scanners accordingly.

"Their complacency will be their ruin," Sang murmured as they moved into the scrubby land beyond the compound.

"It's a human thing, complacency," Ready said, his voice muffled as he kept his head down, watching where he put his feet. Bellona still hung unmoving over his shoulder. The long straight locks of disturbingly blonde hair hung from her head, waving softly with each step Ready took.

"Eriumans are not complacent," Sang said, annoyed.

"They're arrogant," Ready said. "Same thing." He was sounding breathless again.

"I would have checked the monitors constantly," Sang pointed out. "I would have questioned why two new people were there."

"You're not Eriuman, though. Not really."

Sang pressed her lips together to hold back her angry retort. She would need the energy for walking before this day was done.

#

Bellona woke shortly after that and struggled. Ready held her down, while Sang administered the sedative she had tucked away in her pouch. "Are you pleased, now, that I insisted upon contingency planning?" she asked.

Ready scowled and waved away an insect that was trying to lodge on Bellona's face, with its odd, fair skin. "It's one thing to anticipate. It's another to act on every suspicion as if it is fact."

"Now who is refusing to admit they are wrong?"

Ready lifted Bellona up. He didn't speak again until they reached the skiff.

When the skiff was heading for the mainland once more, Sang gave Ready the coordinates for the northern shoreline of the landing field.

He plugged it in and grunted in surprise. "That's the private spaceport."

"Very good."

"That's how you got onto Kachmar? A private ship?"

"How else?"

"Public buses, liners, tourist cruisers, freighters, haulers, day shuttles…" He shrugged, then clutched the side of the skiff as it turned toward the new coordinates. "Did you steal the ship, too?"

"I bought it."

Ready just looked at her.

"I thought it prudent to arrange transport that would allow a second, unregistered person to leave the planet."

Ready look at her, his gaze steady. "So you bought a ship."

"I was provided sufficient funds to cover any possibility."

"Throwing money at a problem to erase guilt." Ready looked away. "The more I hear about Reynard Cardenas, the more I admire him." His tone was withering.

Sang didn't respond. Any response would be a reflection upon the head of her family.

Ready looked down at Bellona, where she lay on the bench between them. "You bought a ship to take her back. Tell me, Sang, was there a single moment anywhere in this where you considered the possibility that you might not get Bellona back?"

"Failure was not a parameter of my assignment."

Ready rolled his eyes. "You thought she was dead."

"Irrelevant."

"So did he."

"Also irrelevant."

"Did *anyone* truly think she might be alive, that this wasn't a magnificent and expensive gesture?"

"Yes."

Surprise skittered across his face. "*That's* who is driving you?"

"Iulia Cardenas Scordina de Carosa is not my employer."

"Just following orders, huh?"

"That is my function."

"Right." Ready turned away, watching the nose of the skiff slice through the black water. "Maybe you should start calling yourself 'we' again."

"I will have to, soon enough," Sang said complacently, looking ahead to where the mainland was a dark bruise on the horizon.

#

Kachmarain City, Kachmar Sodality, The Karassian Homogeny.

Security around the spaceport was nominal, another reason why Sang had chosen to use a private craft. The spaceport administrators considered security to be the responsibility of the ship owners who used the port. Most of the luxury craft did have posted sentries and passive shields, some of them lethal, but the perimeter of the landing field had a simple, sedentary fence. The sea side of the port had nothing at all barring entry, for the coast there was rocky and the seas high.

They wrecked the skiff upon the higher rocks, grounding it more surely than any anchor, then picked their way over to flat ground. Sang carried Bellona until they reached the sleek leisure vehicle, when she handed Bellona back to Ready and disengaged the shielding.

"You bought a Karassian yacht?" Ready asked.

"My registration says I am unenhanced Karassian. I could not arrive in an Eriuman jig."

"This is the Slipstream model. They've been advertising it on almost every stream since I woke up here."

"It is." Sang lowered the ramp and they climbed into the ship.

"Only the best will do, hm?"

"Used vehicles are unreliable, have inquisitive owners and they are, above all, slow." Sang closed up the craft.

The silence inside the ship seemed thick and heavy, after a day at sea with the wind in her ears and nearly three weeks of Karassian screens screaming at her from every angle. Sang pointed. "There is a small medical bay there. Third door."

While Ready laid Bellona on the examination table, Sang connected with the ship's AI and requested a DNA check.

The bed took a sample.

"Confirmed," the computer reported. "Bellona Cardenas Scordina de Deluca."

"You didn't believe me," Ready said, not sounding surprised.

"I am being thorough," Sang told him. She silently asked the computer to prep for departure. The decking shivered under their feet as the engines rumbled to life. The shielding and insulation kept the sound down to a barely heard murmur. Once they were in vacuum, they wouldn't hear it at all.

Sang looked down at the woman lying on the table. It was difficult to equate this very Karassian-looking woman with Max's sister, yet now she was here in front of her, Sang could see even more familiar lines and angles.

"We can't take her back to the family looking this way," Sang said. "They will be horrified."

"Won't they just be happy to have her back?" Ready asked.

Sang discussed it with the computer. "I will take her to Maggar. There is a therapy group there that can reverse the gene expression and return her original appearance."

"You figure it is that easy to go back?" Ready asked.

Sang thought of the days ahead. "It's a start," she admitted. She ordered the bed to secure Bellona's body and keep her sedated, then headed for the door. "I thank you for your assistance, Khalil Ready. You have been of service to the Scordinii and have earned their favor."

"You think I'm leaving?"

She looked back. Ready stood by the table, unmoving. He crossed his arms.

"My next stop is deep inside the Republic," Sang pointed out.

"So?"

"You do not fear crossing that border?" For the first time she wondered where Khalil Ready had come from, before he had been sucked into the Appurtenance Services project.

He ran his fingers down his dark beard. "Do I *look* as if I care?"

Sang hesitated.

"I know. Taking a third person back isn't part of your assignment," Ready said dryly. "Think of it this way. If you don't take me back, you don't get to take Bellona back either. Where I go, she goes."

Sang nodded. "Very well, then. I would advise you to strap in. The inertial filters on this vehicle are sub-standard." She headed for the control deck.

Chapter Five

Primary Healing Complex, Maggar, Eriuman Republic.

It took a long time to wake, to find coherency. Even when she recognized softness beneath her and warmth over her, she still struggled to pull together memories that would tell her where she was. Until then, she kept her eyes closed.

It felt as though she had been asleep for a very long time. There were confusing snatches of memory. Voices, the words not clear. Heat from a sun.

She finally admitted she was not going to be able to put it together here and now. She needed further information. She opened her eyes.

A man sat on a stool, next to an open window. Warm air blew through the window. Sunlight, not harsh, lit the man's face. Dark hair. Thick beard.

She frowned. "Ari..." The name came to her, even though she didn't know this man. Yet as soon as she spoke the name, she knew it was right.

The man took a deep breath and turned to look at her. Pale eyes. "You knew me as Ari, yes. My name—my real name—is Khalil Ready. Your real name...do you remember that?"

"Xenia," she said promptly, then frowned. "No..."

He waited.

"There is something, a long way back." She rolled onto her back and lifted her hand to rub her temple. She paused, her hand in the air. The flesh of her arm was odd. It was perfectly normal skin, yet it didn't look right.

Her movement brought the rest of the room into view. It was a small chamber, enclosed with old-style walls. Soft carpets with muted colors hung on the walls. A bureau by the wide door with ancient-styled drawers looked appropriate for this room, yet equipment sat on the top — sleek, sophisticated, their functions a mystery to the uninitiated.

The terminal next to the bureau was also modern, though styled to look older. The screen showed a display she recognized. It was an array of vital signs.

She looked at her arm again, putting it together. She was the patient.

"Hello, Bellona."

She looked up, recognizing the name. The person who had spoken it stood by the head of her bed, unnoticed until now because of their stillness. She frowned, taking in the copper blond hair and the freckled skin. "I know you."

"We are Sang."

Sang. Max. Mother.

Father!

Bellona gasped, as her identity dropped into place with

the weight of an Eriuman cruiser settling onto a landing pad. It *hurt*. She scrambled to sit up, looking yet again at her arm, which was far too pale to be hers. Her heart ran sickly, the irregular beat making her chest ache.

The terminal beeped furiously.

Ari—*Khalil*—got to his feet. "You're not in danger," he said quickly.

Sang held out their hand. "We're taking you home, as soon as you're ready."

Panic flared, hot and sour. "No!"

"Your family will be overjoyed to see you," Sang added.

"I'm *not* going back there!"

A medical technician hurried into the room. He wore a worried expression.

Sang dropped their hand onto Bellona's shoulder. "You are Bellona Cardenas. You're safe. You're going home."

Bellona gripped Sang's wrist. "You'll have to kill me first." She wrenched the wrist over and at the same time, slammed her hand against the vulnerable elbow. There was a soggy cracking sound. Sang sank to their knees with a gusty, pain-filled groan.

Bellona dropped their wrist, which slid into Sang's lap to rest uselessly.

She scrambled backward, to the other edge of the bed. She clutched at her chest as the pain there bloomed, claiming all of her.

Then there was nothing.

#

A technician pointed Sang toward the courtyard when they asked for Bellona's location. They hurried out to the stone yard, where dead leaves rustled and the sky was gray overhead. All around the yard were verandahs lined with doors to rooms where the practice of healing took place.

Bellona prowled the courtyard like a caged beast, her energy at odds with the peace of the healing house.

Khalil Ready waited as always, his patience undisturbed by her roaming. He sat on one of two chairs that had been placed there for them, his hands woven together and hanging between his knees.

Sang went to Bellona. "You look much more yourself today."

She lifted her arm to look at the back of her hand. "Do I?"

Sang took in her deep olive complexion, the blue eyes and the thick black curls that had been the bane of her life for so many years. "Yes, you do."

Bellona let her hand drop. "I didn't think that was possible."

Khalil lifted his head, as if he had been alerted.

Sang's wariness slid into place, too. "You have been reviewing the footage…" They looked at Khalil, vexed.

"Better she learn it all now," Khalil said quietly. "Or would you rather Bellona trip over the truth somewhere in the future and resent you for not telling her?"

"How could she trip over it? Xenia looked so different.

60

She could have stayed ignorant forever."

Bellona shook her head. "Khalil has been explaining it to me and I have researched for myself. The Karassians use those streams for propaganda. They spread them everywhere, showing the might of the Homogeny to their subjects — the free states, the aligned worlds, anyone they want to intimidate into behaving. Sooner or later, someone will recognize me. There were enough similarities between Xenia and I that speculation would rise, especially now Bellona Cardenas is back from the dead. They will wonder and one day, someone will challenge me on it. It is better I know now and have time to prepare for that. It is better I know what I have done." She looked down at her hands again. "How is your arm?" she added.

Sang held it up and turned their wrist. "It was a minor hurt, easily tended."

"Unlike the lives I took," Bellona muttered.

Sang shifted on their feet. "I have heard from your brother."

The darkness fled from her face. "Max is coming?"

"He says he will be pleased to take you home."

"A naval escort," Khalil said softly. "*That's* a homecoming."

Bellona looked down at her hands again, her pleasure fading. "I must go home, I suppose. I must face them."

Sang felt a touch of alarm. "You must, yes," they said.

"Sang won't rest until they have completed their assignment," Khalil added.

Sang could feel their cheeks heating. "We think only of your mother and your brother...and your father. They must see you again. They must assure themselves that you live, after all."

"Because they have spent the last ten years turning the galaxy inside out, looking for me," Bellona said.

"The war..." Sang said, feeling a rare helplessness.

"There has always been a war," Bellona said shortly.

"I think," Khalil said, "you will find more has changed than has remained the same."

Bellona looked at him, her expression sour. "I have been asleep for ten years. *Nothing* is the same. Not even me."

#

It was difficult to focus upon anything beyond the pain, although when they heard their name being spoken sharply, they roused enough to lift their head.

Khalil Ready was peering at them, a furrow between his brows. This close, Sang could see the brown flecks in his eyes.

"You're sick?" Ready asked. "Why are you sitting on the floor?"

The conditioning to answer when asked a question was strong. Sang reached for and drew the pail closer to their side, moving carefully so the contents did not slosh. "It is convenient, to sit on the floor." The bed the technicians had offered them was too hot beneath their bodies. The walls of the quiet room were cool against their back.

They wrapped their arms about their knees once more. In between the flashes of heat, it was very cold. They shivered.

"What is wrong with you?"

"This is…a natural adjustment."

Ready had been crouching to speak to them. Now he sat and crossed his legs. "You mean, this is what you go through when you drop the gender?"

Sang drew their knees even closer to their chest. The pressure helped. "The technicians assure us this is mild. We were not female long enough to generate organs, which complicates the hormonal rebalance."

"You had breasts," Ready pointed out.

"Increased lactation tissue." Sang paused to ride through another wave of pain. It was a sourceless ache, enveloping their whole body. "Easily reabsorbed."

Ready tilted his head. "Why not just stay a woman?"

"That is not our choice to make. The family rarely assign gender. It complicates everyday concerns that should be simple and elegant. Those given a gender cannot return if they remain gendered for too long."

Ready threaded his fingers together. His thumbs touched. "You do not feel embarrassed, telling me these things?"

"It is a fact, that is all."

"You knew the transition would be like this, then?"

"It is a well understood process."

"Despite knowing, you willingly chose to become female?"

"We could not remain gender neutral and move freely about the Homogeny. They do not give their androids the freedom the Republic does."

Ready's silence was long. "Anything at all, to get Bellona back?"

"That was our assignment."

"Did Reynard Cardenas know what he was asking of you?"

Sang clutched the pail. "You would be best to leave," they gasped.

Ready got to his feet with a lithe movement. "Is there anything that will help?"

Sang leaned over the pail, the nausea swirling. They did not dare speak. The next few moments were uncomfortable and unpleasant. When they were finally capable of taking notice of their environment, they saw that Khalil Ready had left.

There was a fresh cloth and water on the spot where he had sat.

#

The therapists announced that Maximilian's fleet had arrived and were in orbit overhead.

"A whole fleet?" Bellona said.

"Space strategy has changed since you were gone," Sang

told her. "Mostly thanks to your brother."

"What did Max do?"

"He spent years studying the free ships and their political structures. All their ships are small and vulnerable. Any Eriuman cruiser can destroy an entire ship with one cannon shot, not even a volley, yet the free ships constantly hound and evade the cruisers."

"The gnat anomaly, yes," Bellona said impatiently. Then her eyes widened. "Where did I get that from?"

Khalil sat up. "The gnat anomaly is a Karassian expression. They consider freeships to be nothing more than annoying insects, that sometimes sting their military ships. You must have picked it up when you were Xenia."

Bellona swallowed. "On a mission, you mean?"

"Yes."

"Those memories were wiped, you said, to eliminate trauma."

"The active memories, certainly. The base knowledge and expertise they impart cannot be removed without destroying your personality and your ability to function. That is why you were able to bring Sang to their knees, the moment you woke. It is instinctive. Ingrained." He glanced at Sang apologetically, as if he was apologizing for invoking the memory of what she had done to Sang.

Bellona scowled. "What base knowledge and expertise did you acquire while you were an app?"

"I was made an app because of my expertise." Khalil sat

back. "I did nothing but use that expertise, so no new knowledge was acquired."

He was lying. Sang considered calling him out, drawing Bellona's attention to the lie. Only, Khalil had so far worked with good intentions. Sang thought of the cloth and water that had been left for them and said nothing.

Bellona looked at Sang. "My brother studied the freeships...?" she prompted.

Sang nodded. "The freeships were smaller and more maneuverable, their one advantage. Sometimes it is no advantage at all. They sacrifice shielding and null engine size for speed in local space. When they jump, the smaller engine extends the jump double the time a standard Eriuman ship would take, even the heaviest of cruisers. The lighter shielding also makes them vulnerable to holing and radiation excesses."

"It is a matter of strategic priorities," Bellona replied. "What would you rather have on a battlefield? The ability to run away fast, or to be faster while you are fighting?"

"Max chose both," Sang said.

Bellona tilted her head. "To be faster than the freeships and retain the shielding and engine power?" She held up her hand. "Only ships smaller and lighter than the freeships could be faster. The freeships are already operating with minimal shielding and engine size. The only way to be lighter and faster is to drop below minimal safe level."

Sang nodded. "Fast, light, small ships...*tiny* ships, can fit inside bigger ships."

Bellona crossed her arms. "Carriers," she said flatly. "*That* was Max's great innovation? A device that has been used throughout military history?"

Khalil laughed. "Every transport is a carrier of something."

"Max stripped down ship designs, taking away the null engines, the heavy shielding, everything except firepower and room for a pilot. It is not a new idea, but the idea had fallen out of use. When opposing cruisers are even bigger and heavier and more highly armored than your own cruisers, a gnat is useless. Against small ships with minimal shielding, though…" Sang shrugged. "Max was lauded and promoted for his work."

Bellona was still frowning. "The Eriuman Navy is fighting free ships? When did the free states get into the war against the Homogeny?"

Khalil looked at Sang and raised a brow.

"The free states are not at war with either the Homogeny or the Republic," Sang said carefully.

"Eriuman and Karassia have never declared war, either," Bellona shot back, "yet they've been enemies since before I was born. Why is Max shooting at freeships?"

"He isn't," Sang said quickly. "At least, not unless they shoot first, or they're in Eriuman territory without authorization. He patrolled the borders of the Republic for many years, where he developed his theories. Now, he uses the personal fighters to harass the Karassian ships."

"A gnat against a giant? How does that work?" There was no sarcasm in her voice, just strong interest.

"I am sure Max will explain that to you in detail," Sang assured her.

Bellona rolled her eyes. "*You* tell me, Sang. Max doesn't think I'm interested in war."

"*Are* you interested?" Sang asked curiously. "Max often told me you did not like to talk about such matters."

"I *am* such matters now, aren't I?"

#

As was proper, Sang stood at the back of the reception room, while Bellona and the head therapist stood at the front, waiting for Max and his officers to arrive. Bellona wore a borrowed dress that swirled around her ankles. She was bereft of jewelry. Her hair had been piled upon the top of her head but tendrils had escaped. She was a messy echo of many moments Sang could recall from the past. Family dinners, greeting lines, assemblies, parties, seasonal celebrations.

Khalil did not stand at the back with Sang. Neither did he take a place at the front where, as the hero who had rescued the Cardenas family's long lost daughter, he had a right to stand. He wore black and stood off to one side, the observer's position.

Most of the healers, therapists, technicians and aides were also waiting in the big stone room to see the son and heir of the Cardenas family and to enjoy this small piece of pageantry. They talked among themselves in quiet tones, until the rap of boots on the verandah outside alerted them.

Bellona kept her gaze on the door. Her chin was up, yet she did not smile.

The first officers through the door were junior grade. The people in the room stepped silently aside, forming a ragged corridor to the top.

Max was next, with a tail of officers and aides behind him. He turned his head as soon as he stepped inside, searching for Bellona. When he saw her, he smiled. It was an easy smile, bereft of any ceremony and full of warmth.

Sang was startled. They had not seen Max in person for many years, only by screens and quick communications when Max needed personal affairs dealt with on Cardenas. He had matured since his last visit home and not just in age. His shoulders had filled out, giving him the family silhouette of tall, broad-shouldered men with square jaws and direct gazes. He had shorn his hair to a neat stubble. Yet the change was not purely physical. He was at ease with himself. Confidence radiated from him. He was comfortable enough in this room of strangers and his fellow, more junior officers, to show his feelings for his sister.

When he reached her, he did not wait for the formal acknowledgements to be completed, either. He pushed past his officer and swept Bellona up in his arms and held her for a long moment, before putting her back on her feet and studying her at arm's length.

The officers all stood rigidly at attention, waiting for a cue that would tell them how to react and what to do. Max had by-passed what was familiar to them.

"You haven't changed. Not at all," Max declared.

"The therapists are very good."

His smile faded. "At the surface level, I'm sure they are."

Bellona stepped out of his reach. "We should talk."

The last of his good humor vanished. Max nodded. "We should." He looked around, spotted the senior therapist and director of the complex, Riorden, a man with no hair and oddly pale eyes, marking him as a member of one of the minor clans.

"Is there any chance of a meal that isn't assembled?" Max asked him. "Every meal I've had for nearly a year was identical to the last."

The director murmured to one of his aides, who hurried from the room. Then Riorden bowed and indicated that Max and Bellona should follow him. Sang silently approved of the man's sensitivity toward rank. Medics were often sticky about such things. Riorden, though, was showing proper deference.

Max spoke to his officers, who stepped back almost in unison.

Max and Bellona followed the director from the room. Sang followed. Max would need them while separated from his officers. Their glance met Khalil's.

As Bellona's rescuer, Ready should have a seat at the meal table. Sang beckoned to him.

The director showed them into the common room and over to the top end of the long table the senior therapists used. There was no one else using the room, leaving four other long tables empty and bare.

Three kitchen staff were laying the end of the table, their faces red and their movements hurried. Max nodded at them and took the seat at the end of the table.

The director chose the chair on his right.

Sang waited for Bellona and Khalil to sit before quietly lifting one of the chairs from the middle of the long table, putting it against the wall and lowering themselves onto it. It would keep them close at hand, yet wouldn't draw attention to themselves as standing might.

Khalil stared at them. He was frowning again.

Sang gave him a reassuring smile and turned their gaze away deliberately. Khalil needed to concentrate on the conversation to come.

Max was looking at Khalil, too. "Given that you sit at my table and next to my sister, I would presume that you are Ready, the man who found her?"

Khalil got to his feet and gave a short nod of his head. It was almost a bow, only not quite. The movement looked unpracticed. "Khalil Ready."

Max sat back in his chair. The movement looked expansive and open, yet it also cleared his right hip. His hand stayed on the table, the fingers in a relaxed curl. It put his hand within a short drop to his hip. There was no visible weapon there, only Sang was familiar with the discipline and practices of the Navy. There would be a weapon within reach, somewhere on Max's body. A miniature ghostmaker or perhaps a simple knife — one properly weighted for throwing.

Bellona recognized the deceptive shift of Max's chair for what it really was, for she put her hand on the table in entreaty. "Max, Khalil saved my life. He sent the message to Father. He is not our enemy."

Khalil did not move. Perhaps he recognized the unspoken danger.

Riorden, the director, looked from face to face, puzzlement stitched to his own.

"You are not Eriuman," Max said.

"No."

"Nor are you Karassian."

Khalil smiled. "I was born a free-stater. My loyalties have shifted since I emerged from the app program."

"You fight for Erium now?" Max asked. There was a dangerous silkiness to his voice.

"I am not a fighter," Khalil said honestly, "and I do not consider Erium to be my enemy."

"A neuter, then?"

"Max, enough," Bellona snapped. "I vouch for him. That is all you need to know."

Max glanced at her, a shadow of surprise passing over his face.

Bellona slapped the table with her hand, lightly. "You should be gracious and thank Khalil for getting me out of that place. No one in the family managed it."

This time, Max's astonishment lingered.

Bellona kept her gaze steady and waited.

Max cleared his throat. "Khalil Ready, you have my thanks for returning my sister to Erium."

Khalil nodded.

"Please, sit."

Khalil glanced at Bellona. She nodded and he settled back on his chair.

Max watched the interchange, his eyes narrowing.

The kitchen staff reappeared, this time carrying trays with plates and cups. The breakfast Max had precipitously demanded had arrived.

It appeared that Max had not been lying about his need for real food. He tackled his bowl of stranglers and greens as if the meal might be taken from him at any instant. He kept his head down, with no attempt at conversation.

Bellona glanced at Sang. Sang could understand her disorientation. No family meal had ever been so silent.

As the midday meal had been served only a short while ago, everyone but Max picked at their food. Max did not seem to notice the silence. He finished the bowl, pushed it aside and reached for the coffee mug, then sat back again.

This time, it was simply a backward thrust of his chair away from the table.

"My thanks," he told the director. "They say assembled food is no different from dirt-grown, yet after a while I yearn for the flavors of home."

"Maggar is not Cardenas, but we try," Riordan said. "I am pleased you find it to your satisfaction."

Bellona put down her fork. "Tell me how your little fighting ships tackle a Karassian frigate."

Max almost choked on his coffee. He coughed to clear his throat and put the mug down again. He gave her a small smile. "I hardly think naval strategies and tactics is a suitable subject for the dining table."

"I have no family news to discuss," Bellona said. "They say you are a hero, Max. I want to understand why. How are you defeating them?"

Max picked invisible crumbs from his sleeve. "There will be plenty of time to talk about such matters on the return to Cardenas," he said, "when we're behind closed doors and secure." His gaze flickered toward the director.

"I should go..." Riordon got to his feet.

"No, don't," Max said curtly. "We were about to speak of arrangement to leave, in which you will be involved."

Riordan hesitated, then sat back down again.

"Then you really are taking me back to Cardenas?" Bellona asked.

"That is why I and a good part of the fleet are here."

Bellona considered him for a moment. "I'm not going back."

"Of course you are. Where else would you go?"

"Somewhere. I don't know yet."

Max studied her. "You've tried running before. Look where it got you."

Bellona glanced at Riordan and Khalil. Then she met Max's gaze. "It will be different this time."

"How?" Max demanded. "You're one of the most notorious people in the galaxy now. You think there isn't a single soul, free-stater, Karassian or Eriuman, who doesn't know who Xenia is? The Homogeny saturated the known worlds with Xenia's triumphs."

"That wasn't me." Bellona's tone was calm, but her jaw had tightened.

"Explain that to the families of Xenia's victims."

Bellona paled. "That is a part of my plan," she said quietly.

Max made an impatient sound. "*What* plan? There is nowhere you can go where you will not be recognized and pilloried for the suffering you have caused, except Erium."

Bellona swallowed. "You say that because you feel guilty."

Khalil looked at Max sharply, his eyes narrowed.

"I have nothing to feel guilty about," Max said flatly.

"You helped me leave Cardenas. You found the free ship."

Max pressed his lips together. Then he squared his shoulders. "I can't help that a Karassian patrol found the ship. Wang was a superior captain."

"The Karassians grabbed the ship as soon as it came out of null space," Bellona replied. "It was almost as if they knew the *Hathaway* would be there."

Max grew still. "Are you implying I told the Karassians?"

Bellona considered him for a long moment. "No," she said at last. "Someone did, though. Someone from inside the family who knew where I was."

"Why would *anyone* do that?" Max demanded, his voice low.

Sang leaned forward, their interest sharpening. When Max had been still living on Cardenas, before joining the Navy, he had shared everything with Sang. The frankness had helped Sang be a better assistant. Bellona had disappeared ten years ago, shortly before Max had left. Sang had considered the possibility that the two events were connected but had not pursued the line of enquiry because it concerned Max, who rightfully got to decide what Sang did or did not need to know about his life. This was the first time Sang had caught a glimpse of supporting evidence and along with it, the implication that Max had not told Sang everything he had known about Bellona's disappearance.

Max had not told *anyone*. So who had known Bellona had stolen away on a freeship?

Max shrugged. "It could simply have been unfortunate

timing. The *Hathaway* was an old ship, badly masked."

"An old, clunky freeship is what you used to help your sister?" Khalil asked.

Max looked at him. "I couldn't put her on an Eriuman cruiser, could I?"

Riordan cleared his throat. "Really, I should be going…" He got to his feet and this time he did not wait for Max to order him to sit down again. He hurried from the room, his relief painting itself on his face.

Bellona glanced at Riordan's retreating back. She brought her gaze back to Max. "I can head for the free states. I don't look like Xenia anymore. I can disappear there."

"You look enough like her that someone will recognize you," Max assured her.

"Really? Then in all the time the Karassians were plastering Xenia across the galaxy, why did you not see it was me?"

Khalil touched her wrist.

Bellona sat back with a sigh.

"I thought you were dead," Max said flatly. "Destroyed along with Wang and her people. I saw the wreckage, Bellona. I spent a week pulling frozen bodies out of vacuum and matching them. When I didn't find you, I presumed I simply hadn't looked hard enough. The area had already been annexed by the Karassians. I was forced to leave. So no, when I saw Xenia, I never once thought it might be you. It just wasn't a possibility. Only, now I know what Xenia looks like, I can see her in you." His jaw flexed. "So will everyone else."

His voice was harsh.

Bellona pressed her lips together. "You're taking me back to Cardenas no matter what, aren't you?"

"You're safer there, dear sister." Max grimaced. "You are right, I carry guilt for my part in what happened to you. I won't risk it happening again."

"I can take care of myself," Bellona said.

"That's what you said, ten years ago," Max said. "I believed you then, which was my mistake." He got to his feet. "We lift in six hours. Be ready."

Chapter Six

Primary Healing Complex, Maggar, Eriuman Republic.

Sang prepared for what would happen next.

Barely two hours later, Bellona strode into the room Riordon had lent to Max to use as an office until the fleet's departure. There had been a steady stream of military personnel in and out of the office since Max had sat behind the desk. Bellona's arrival was noticed only by Sang, where they stood behind the desk. She had changed out of the dress. Her trousers and boots were plain and simple. Her hair was down once more, the curls shoved back over her shoulder. She was scowling.

Through the open door, Sang could see Khalil leaning on the stone parapet that separated the central courtyard from the deep verandah.

The moment Sang had anticipated had arrived.

Bellona stopped in front of the desk. "Your officer… Henley. He tells me Khalil is denied passage on the *Decimus.*"

Max dismissed the screen in front of him. "He's a freestater with questionable loyalties, Bellona. I can't let him aboard an Eriuman military cruiser."

"I don't question his loyalties."

"You're not Navy, either."

Bellona's scowl deepened. "You and Father made sure of that, didn't you?"

Max got to his feet. "You're being unreasonable."

Sang moved around the desk and stepped out of the door. Khalil straightened as Sang moved over to him.

"Do *you* want passage to Cardenas?" Sang asked quietly. Behind them, Bellona's and Max's voices rose, the tones strident.

Khalil glanced through the open doorway once more. "Bellona wants me with her. That is reason enough to go."

Sang nodded. "We must take the ship we purchased to Cardenas, for Reynard to decide what must be done with it. We have already begun jump preparations. You can travel with us."

Khalil narrowed his eyes. "Max won't like that."

Sang pushed away the troubling thought. "Possibly."

"So why do it?"

Sang considered. "Until Bellona is presented to her father, our task is not complete. We must work to ensure that meeting happens. If that means catering to her wishes, then we will."

Khalil's mouth turned up. There was a warm glow in his eyes. "Or you could say you're doing it for Bellona. I won't tell anyone."

Sang stared at him, confusion making their thoughts

churn. "We…belong to Max."

"Yes, you do," Khalil agreed. "I accept your offer of passage to Cardenas, Sang. Thank you."

#

Sang spoke to Bellona after she emerged from Max's office, her jaw set.

She received the news with growing calm. "Why didn't you interrupt us and tell us this? Why wait until now?"

Sang hesitated. "Max would not appreciate what we have done."

"I'll tell him it was my idea," Bellona said. "He's already furious with me. Nothing changes, does it Sang? Max always hated being the younger."

"He loves you," Sang said quickly.

"He loved the memory of me more." Her smile was rueful. "Now I am back, he is determined to be a perfect Eriuman to make me look bad." She rested her hand on Sang's arm. "While you are in-transit, could you do something for me?"

"We?"

It was her turn to look doubtful. "Do you mind? I won't have access to a terminal on Max's ship. I'll be locked up in a hastily cleared-out stateroom with nothing to do but look pretty and charm the officers."

Sang suspected it was an accurate estimation. Navy ships were not used to civilian passengers. They wouldn't know what to do with her. It was only because Bellona was the Cardenas' daughter and Max's sister that the rare privilege had been offered.

"We do not mind," Sang told her. "We will have little to do, too." The as-yet-unnamed yacht was just as fast as the lumbering *Decimus*, which had to match its pace with the slowest convoyer in the fleet, yet the jump would still take days.

Bellona half-closed her eyes. "Remember these names. Aideen, Fontana, Hayes, Thecla, Hero, Retha, Vang." She opened her eyes again. "Do you have them?"

"Yes. What should we do with them?"

"Research them. They are as I was, Sang. They're still in there. Still being used. I *think*." She grimaced and touched her temple. "Perhaps I have imagined them all."

"If you did not, there would be traces," Sang said. "Images, footage, reports. If even one other name appears somewhere, it would confirm they are not your imagination."

"I want to know if those memories are real."

"Ari is real."

Bellona drew in a breath and let it out. "He gives me hope that the rest is just as real. Find out for me, Sang. I would be grateful."

#

Xindaria (Xindar III), Free Space City State.

Ferid perched on the polished tabletop, staring down at the body and the blood soaking into the handwoven rug beneath, darkening the pleasing pattern and disturbing the symmetry.

He had grabbed the man right off the quiet, tree-lined street and pulled him into the nearest little house, obeying an instinct that said to act at once, for it would be unpredictable and unexpected.

Ferid had obeyed the instinct. No one had seen him. No one had noticed a thing.

He had followed the man for four days, using scans from low orbit. In this bucolic place, with its unenhanced humans and peasant lifestyle, Ferid would have been noticed. His implants would have drawn attention. Instead, he had stayed on his ship and scanned. The scans had made the task challenging.

Ferid couldn't remember the name of the man now. He had run Arany's navigation systems for years, until shrapnel had taken off his left leg below the knee. Arany had set the man up with a house on this maddeningly simple planet. Ferid did not understand why. The man was no longer useful and should have been killed once a replacement had been found. Arany's failure to remove him was a weakness Ferid had exploited.

Only the man had proved to be as stubborn and closed-mouth as the girl on Pushyan.

Now Ferid was staring at another lifeless form, wondering if he needed to reconsider his tactics. Was there a way to make these people talk that he had failed to consider?

His brooding gaze drifted over the arrangement of images on the cupboard front, next to the table. Children. Gap-toothed, ugly, noisy.

Families.

Ferid stirred, as his mind moved in dusty areas of knowledge.

The people he had spoken to were ferociously loyal to Arany. They had easily given up their lives to protect Arany. What if they were given a different alternative? What if they were faced with a choice of talking or losing not *their* lives, but the life of someone closer to them than Arany himself?

Ferid jumped off the table, happy once more and also vexed he had not thought of this weeks ago. Although, he was a vastly talented, highly tuned artist who required unsullied thought to do his work. Yes, that was why the emotional baggage of free-state unenhanced humans had not entered his mind.

He was flexible, though. He would adapt.

#

Karassian Luxury Yacht, Maggar-Cardenas, Null-Space.

There was ample spare time on the jump to Cardenas to dig into the war archives to see if any of the names on Bellona's list were to be found there. The yacht was Karassian so the archives on the exploits of their war heroes would be more complete than any Eriuman databases. Sang occupied themselves with the research, while Khalil took advantage of the yacht's adequate movement room.

On the third and last day of the jump, Khalil dropped onto the bench opposite Sang and looked at the screen Sang had displayed.

"I know him," Khalil said. "That's Hayes."

"So I have discerned," Sang said in agreement.

Khalil studied the image. Hayes was an enhanced monster, a head higher than the tallest Eriuman soldier in the unit he was destroying, with a heavy forehead over ferocious eyes, powerful shoulders and metal hands that deflected the beams from ghostmakers back at the firer. The image was a still one, showing Hayes in mid-air, just after launching himself at the remains of the unit, one hand up to deflect a beam, the other reaching for the nearest neck. The caption was an excited recitation of the numbers of Eriuman he had killed before the image had been captured and how many more he killed after that, as he took control of a grounded Eriuman convoyer.

"Hayes thought his hands were for gardening, to let him dig the earth barehanded," Khalil said. "He spent hours, kneeling in dirt. He was proud of the pine-lilies most of all."

Sang looked at the monster, at the hands reaching out. "Bellona's memories are real, then. She was not imagining her friends."

Khalil grimaced. "They, on the other hand, do not even realize she has gone."

"It is better so."

"Is it?"

Sang closed down the screen. "For now. You wish to speak with us?"

"Maybe I just want company."

Sang did not dignify the response with an answer.

Khalil smiled, showing his very white teeth. "You are combat trained."

"We have monitored three years of combat training, but we are not trained."

"Whose training?"

Sang hesitated, weighing up conflicting privacy concerns. "The training was arranged for Max, which is why we monitored, yet Bellona also trained."

Khalil smiled. "Were you a monitor or a benign sentry? I have a feeling that Bellona's family would not have approved of her training."

"They did not." Sang shut up.

Khalil stroked his beard thoughtfully. "You realize that her training was probably why the Karassians used her as an app instead of parading her around as a useless Eriuman hostage before publicly executing her?"

Sang drew in a breath and let it out. "The thought had occurred to me." It was not an easy thought.

"Combat training," Khalil said, pulling the subject back.

"You're trained well enough to be useful. I want you to train me."

"You are not a warrior."

"Neither was Max, or Bellona, once."

Sang considered him. "You have survived without combat skills until now. Does your arrival in Eriuman space have something to do with the sudden need to be able to defend yourself?"

Khalil didn't move. "I do not fool myself that I will be welcome there. In a room full of Eriuman primary clan members, only Bellona will consider me a friend."

"We consider you an ally."

Khalil grimaced. "But not a friend. As long as I am useful, Sang, you will tolerate me. You have learned the biases of your family well."

Sang did not deny it. "Family intrigues are usually political in nature. They prefer that blood only be shed for reasons of war."

"The politics, I can handle. It's the exceptions I must prepare for. Why did Bellona consider it prudent to learn combat skills?"

"For many reasons. Because Max was training and she was not. Because she wished to go to war. Because her father said she could not."

"Ah."

Sang tilted their head the way that Khalil sometimes did, when he was assessing a situation. "You risk much, simply because Bellona wishes you nearby."

"Yes," Khalil said flatly. His gaze met Sang's, steady and frank.

"Why?" Sang demanded.

Khalil's gaze dropped to his hands. "Did you know that Xenia, when she was in Ledan, thought she was a dancer? She loved the idea that she was pleasing others with her dancing, even though she couldn't actually remember a performance. She didn't mind the aches and pains, the casts, the injuries. She considered them part of her work. The Xenia that I knew — that Ari knew — was gentle. Creative. They took that away from her, the Karassians, in their effort to forge a hero." His gaze flickered up to meet Sang's. "Her family are doing the same thing."

"You don't know that," Sang protested. "You have only met Max."

"There is a reason she left Erium ten years ago, Sang. Do you know what it is?"

"No one does, except for Bellona."

"She does not know either. I asked her." Khalil looked at Sang directly once more. "She remembers fighting the Karassians when they boarded the *Hathaway*. She remembers killing at least one of them, bare-handed. She also remembers Max getting her on the freeship, while everything before that is gone."

"Trauma," Sang breathed. "Yet the memory must be buried or she would not be so reluctant to return."

Khalil nodded. "Therefore, I find it prudent to acquire combat skills."

"There is only a day left before we arrive at Cardenas."

"I do not expect to learn what I must in one day," Khalil said, his smile brief.

"We only mention the remaining time because there is more urgent need you must address, first."

Khalil lifted his brow. "Oh?"

"From our long experience with the Scordini family, we guess that Bellona's return will generate much…pomp."

Khalil ran a hand down the neutral black tunic over trousers that he favored. They were bereft of any ornamentation. "I will be at the back wall with you, Sang. This will do."

Sang shook their head. "It is not a chance you should take. If you are included in the ceremony, then you must appear to be one of them. An equal. Such things matter to the family."

"I won't dress up in colors and gilt just to make them happy."

"You should not," Sang agreed. "Instead, you should make your own mark."

Khalil let his hand drop. "You have an idea, then."

"We do."

Chapter Seven

Cardenas (Findlay IV), Findlay System, Eriuman Republic.

The Great Hall was a stand-alone structure in the center of the city. The city itself had a name that most people had forgotten. As the seat of power for the Cardenas family, the most senior family in the primary Scordini clan, the city had become known as Cardenas, just as the planet was named. The city had sprung up around the functions of the family, with structures that included the Great Hall.

When the ground cars that had been sent to pick up the new arrivals at the family's private landing field had headed for the city center, instead of the homebase on the hill to the north, Sang knew their guess had been right. There would be a formal welcome ceremony at the Great Hall.

As they pulled up, Khalil studied the screen in front of him. "They're all family? Everyone out there?"

"Everyone on Cardenas is connected to the family in one way or another. This is a family event, yes."

"There are thousands of them."

"Yes."

Khalil glanced down at his new finery. It was black, a tunic and trousers, with a more formal long coat over the top. Glitter and gilt was absent, while a subdued length of piping followed the style lines, which had been all Khalil would tolerate. "Anything more is a distraction."

"Elegance is often used in such a way," Sang pointed out as they worked on the print file, preparing it.

"I meant *I* would be distracted. No, Sang. Enough."

The ground car halted and Khalil shifted his feet, preparing to exit. Sang gripped his wrist, staring at the screen. "Wait."

Khalil protested. Sang pointed at the screen.

There were two more ground vehicles drifting through the pack of people toward the Great Hall, their armored fields glinting in the early morning sunshine.

"Who?" Khalil asked.

"I believe one has Max and Bellona. The other, senior members of the family." Sang watched.

"Max and Bellona go first?" Khalil guessed.

"Yes."

"Then we're definitely last."

His dry tone made Sang smile.

The first car opened and Max stepped out and waved as everyone cheered and clapped. He reached back and helped Bellona out. She was appropriately dressed in a green gown, although for the second time, she had eschewed jewelry. Her hair was down. She did not wave, even when the cheering grew louder.

Sang remembered the Karassian officer forcing Xenia to wave.

The second vehicle opened and a tall man emerged. "That is Max and Bellona's uncle, Gaubert," Sang told Khalil. Gaubert waved to the crowd, then helped a woman from the vehicle. "The woman in gleaming red is his wife, Thora," Sang added.

Gaubert brushed down his braided jacket, then led Thora to where Max and Bellona were standing at the foot of the stairs.

"Now you must exit," Sang said. "Go to Bellona at once."

Khalil raised his brow, but obeyed. He walked straight over to Bellona, who gave him a stiff, self-conscious smile. As Sang got out, they kept their gaze on Khalil as Max murmured to him. Khalil nodded.

Max held out his hand to Bellona, who took it. Together, they climbed the stairs. Khalil fell in behind them, with Gaubert and Thora following.

The people watching them enter the Great Hall swept in behind them, keen to enter as soon as possible so they would not miss a moment of the pageantry. Sang edged their way between people, careful to not bump or push anyone. Progress up the stairs was slow as the numbers were many. As soon as the lintel of the big doors passed overhead, Sang nudged out of the flow and climbed the service stairs to the balcony that ran the width of the back of the hall. As a member of the inner family, Sang was allowed to pass through the security shields. There was no one on the balcony, for everyone who would be permitted access to the balcony was standing on the high dais at the front of the hall, or was walking the long length of the hall toward the dais.

Reynard Cardenas waited at the front of the dais, wearing the family colors, his wide shoulders made wider by the formal coat and high collar. His expression was impassive, his gaze unmoving. The plane of his brow was unfurrowed. Only the short hair that he wore brushed forward showed any sign of frailty, for it was shot with gray. He appeared to be watching the small party walking along the aisle, himself a still rock of a man on the higher dais.

Iulia was a pace behind him. She glowed with joy, her gaze on Max and Bellona. She held her hands tightly in front of her.

Ranged behind the two were the more senior members of the family, those closest to Reynard in either blood or favor.

Applause, shouting and cheering filled the hall. Sang sampled the sounds. Analyzed them. There were no sour notes to be detected. As usual, the city was as pleased to celebrate the family occasion as the family itself appeared to be.

Max climbed the steps up to the dais. Instead of moving a step ahead of Bellona, which was usual, he stayed abreast of her. Once on the dais, he turned and presented Bellona to Reynard with a flourish. The theatricality was a new element. Had Max finally learned to move within the family strictures for maximum personal freedom? His success with the Eriuman Navy would certainly indicate as much. This was another sign.

As Reynard took his daughter's hand from Max, the noise in the hall leapt higher. Sang glanced from one upturned, shining face to the next. Everyone was overjoyed at Bellona's return.

Then Max stepped aside and waved Khalil forward. Khalil moved up next to Bellona and Reynard held out his hand. Khalil, uncoached, followed suit. So Reynard grasped his elbow and drew him forward in a formal hug and patted his shoulder, then released him.

They were talking. Sang could see their lips moving, only the sound in the hall was thunderous.

Reynard turned to the audience and held up Bellona's hand.

The cheering intensified.

Bellona attempted a smile. Sang could see her mouth working as she tried. The pulse at the base of her throat fluttered wildly, but the smile did not form.

#

After the formal public ceremony, a private family function was scheduled at the homebase on the high hill overlooking the city. A dozen ground cars carried the invited guests up the hill. Inside the grounds, help-meets were waiting with mulled wine in tall cups, for the chill of winter still gripped the city, even though the snow had gone.

Sang passed into the house without partaking, for it was no longer their role to blend in. There was a mild relief in returning to familiar behavior patterns, even though most of the more recent habits had been built around the absence of Maximilian. It would require concentration to restore the focus now Max had returned, even temporarily.

Sang moved into the big gathering area, that was open to the elements on three sides to take advantage of the view down into the valley and the city lights. They checked arrangements for hosting guests were in place. The help-meets and aides that were not handing out refreshments at the entrance were here, arranging the sideboards with more cups, more aromatic wine and hot food.

The fields were still up, so the interior of the room was warm. Sang took note and went back out to the entryway. Max and Bellona were just passing through, with Khalil following closely behind.

Sang helped Max out of his coat. He was still in uniform, which was appropriate for this hour. Sang would check to see if the civilian clothing he had left behind was laundered and wearable, although the shirts would all have to be reprinted to accommodate Max's increased dimensions in the upper body. As Max chatted easily with cousins and friends, Sang visually measured his proportions and hurried back to Max's old suite to compare them against the stored clothing.

Once Max's immediate wardrobe needs had been dealt with, Sang returned to the gathering room.

Everyone was inside now. To accommodate the number, most of the seating had been removed and guests swirled about the room in easy-moving patterns. A gathering of this size was unusual. There were second cousins from off-world here, as well as the more immediate uncles and aunts and first cousins.

Reynard took up his favorite position in the corner of the room where two pillars held up the roof and where the light was greatest during the day. At night, directional lighting also picked out the corner. A quirk of field technology and the intersection of two fields made the corner snug and comfortable no matter what the weather may be on the other side of the fields.

Although there was nothing as crass as a line of people waiting to speak to Reynard as the head of the family, there was a steady flow of people seeking him out in his corner, to exchange a few words, to thank him for the invitation and to add another tiny layer to their relationship as a hedge against future politics.

There was another invisible line waiting to speak to Bellona, although this one was shorter. Bellona sat upon the only chair in the room, a high one that kept her at the same level as those speaking to her.

Sang noticed that Khalil had gravitated to the back of the room. No one sought his company, so Sang went over and stood next to him for a short moment.

"I'm wondering when either of them will speak to the

other," Khalil said, crossing his arms. "They could still be on different planets, right now."

"There is a timing to such things," Sang said.

Khalil rolled his eyes. "She's his daughter. Why must there be a right time?"

"There are still too many cousins and distant family in the room for an intimate conversation."

Khalil's smile was knowing. "Even if it was just the two of them, it would still be too many people." He nodded his head. "They cannot possibly see each other, not with this many people, yet they are both fully aware of the other."

Sang considered the arrangement of people in the room. They narrowed their focus upon Reynard. Reynard was always formally polite when more than the immediate family were nearby, yet there was a stiffness about his stance tonight that Sang had first assumed to be tiredness.

Bellona had found a way to smile, but it was not a warm expression. Even though she sat, her back was very straight. In between smiling, her jaw flexed.

A voice rose from among the polite chatter. "Of course she was abducted! The Karassians took her, right from under our noses!"

The voice was Iulia's. She held a small court of her own, mostly women of the family, with some partners in tow, over by the smaller sideboard where the wine samovar steamed.

At her protest, Max spun on his heels to look at his mother. He was on the far side of the room, with a small group of cousins. His turn sent his elbow into the side of a help-meet, who just barely controlled the tray of used cups they were carrying. The cups toppled with damp chimes, but Max didn't look. He was staring at his mother.

"How dare you suggest otherwise, Magdalena!" Iulia cried.

Soft voices tried to shush her, to turn the subject.

"My daughter did not run away!"

Bellona didn't move. She was a frozen pillar of flesh, her gaze on her hands.

Conversations checked. Heads turned.

Reynard beckoned to Riz, Iulia's personal assistant. Riz hurried over and bent their head to listen to Reynard's quiet command. They nodded and hurried back to Iulia, to whisper in her ear.

"No, I will not retire," Iulia said, her voice still loud enough to be heard everywhere in the room.

Max was standing as still as Bellona was sitting. His hands were tight fists.

Reynard's face might have been carved from the same marble as the pillars on either side of him. As much as it was possible for his deeply olive skin to show white, it was. Pale strips of flesh bracketed his mouth. The scar stood out.

"Tension is causing interesting reactions, isn't it?" Khalil murmured.

A tight knot of family members surrounded Iulia, drowning her voice in soft concern. The heads drew together. Then, with Riz among them, the group drifted toward the arch that led into the interior. Iulia was being removed.

Sang went over to Max and waited.

Max glanced at them. His shoulders relaxed. His fingers uncurled.

"Perhaps this would be a good moment to change out of your uniform?" Sang suggested. "A general movement out of the room would be...supportive."

Max nodded, yanking at the high collar. "Exactly what I was thinking. Watch Bellona, while I am gone." He turned and stalked from the room, as many of the family members were, as if Iulia's departure had been a natural phase in the proceedings.

Reynard was already speaking to someone else. His pallor was fading.

Bellona, though, had not relaxed. No one sought her out. She sat alone, as if her mother's outburst had made her radioactive. Sang obeyed Max's last order and moved over to her. Khalil beat Sang there.

"That is what they think of me," Bellona said, her voice low. "That I ran away, like a coward."

"You don't know what happened. You can say that truthfully," Khalil assured her.

"I remember Max taking me off the planet, though." Bellona dropped her voice even lower. "I wasn't abducted from here."

"Did Max tell you why you left?" Khalil asked.

"We barely talked," Bellona said. She grimaced. "The life of a captain is apparently a frantic one."

"Perhaps you should ask him, now that he is home."

Bellona sighed. "If I get the chance."

"Perhaps you will need to manufacture the opportunity," Sang said.

Khalil nodded. "Your family doesn't like talking about difficult subjects. You'll have to nail Max to the ground."

Bellona's mouth lifted in a barely suppressed smile that held a wicked glint. "*That* is something I can do, now."

#

Iulia's departure signaled more than just a natural pause. Sang catalogued faces and saw that many of the fringe relatives did not return to the gathering.

The numbers in the gathering room thinned. The volume of conversation dropped. Max returned and his civilian clothing audibly approved of by cousins. Reynard waved him over and pressed his hand on Max's shoulder, his fingers gripping tightly, as Reynard spoke to Gaubert and Markjohn, the youngest of the brothers. Max and Reynard were the same height, which had not been the case when Max had left.

Sang hovered near Max's elbow. The peculiar tensions in the evening had jolted something in the man. When he returned to the gathering room, Max drank several glasses of the mulled wine quickly, then drained more at a steadier pace. Sang could foresee need of their services and waited.

Soon enough, Max was swaying. Sang stole the cup from his unsteady fingers, handed it to another aide and slid under Max's arm and straightened. Reynard pretended not to notice, although his jaw was tight even as he spoke. Gaubert and Markjohn merely looked amused. It wasn't unusual for at least one person to overindulge at family gatherings, although it was rarely Reynard's immediate family.

Sang helped Max stagger to his bed, peeled off his boots and arranged him in a fashion that would not tax tendons or muscles if he fell asleep in that position.

"She doesn' trust him," Max muttered. "I don' understand."

Sang was in complete agreement, which bothered them as much as it had appeared to bother Max, although for different reasons. Max just wanted everyone to get along. He never had liked family arguments, even those not involving him, for Reynard drove most of the conflict.

Sang sealed the suite against casual entrances, a timed key to their prints only and set to expire at a reasonable hour tomorrow morning. They went back to the gathering room. By now, most of the extended family would be gone, except perhaps for Reynard's brothers and sisters. It would be possible to tidy and clean and not get in the way of the family while doing it.

The short day was growing dim, which put the airy rooms inside the house into deeper twilight. The help-meets had not added light to the public rooms. It was not yet an issue to navigate through the big spaces, especially for those familiar with every piece of furniture and carpet.

There were pockets of conversation all through the house. Family had drawn together in twos and threes, away from the gathering room, to talk quietly. Sang did not try to hear any of the conversations. Tones were light, interspersed with laughter, highlighted by happy notes.

The library was the last room before the gathering room. Sang had never understood why the room was named such. It did not contain books, nor shelves to hold ancient tomes upon them. It was the grandly formal reception room where Reynard Cardenas did most of his working and thinking. There was one comfortable chair and several less comfortable visitor chairs, glowing carpets on the walls and little else. Wait, Reynard's aging assistant, supplied all computing functions, communications and security when there was a visitor.

When Reynard was not working in the room, it was a silent, almost featureless place except for the single big green armchair, which provided the only point of focus.

There was someone in the room when Sang moved quietly past the wide doorway. Sang glanced only to ascertain they were not interfering with Reynard's possessions, then moved on smartly, startled. In that brief glance, they saw more than enough.

The image lingered, though. Bellona and Khalil, standing close. His hand moving softly against her throat. Bellona reaching for him, her face turned up, every line of her body speaking of want, matching Khalil's tense need.

Sang moved as quietly as possible out into the gathering room, where the light was much brighter and the sound of conversation, clinking cups and plates drowned out the silence they left behind.

They felt no surprise. The fact merely confirmed what they had subconsciously concluded. They felt neither pleasure nor dismay at the confirmation. Instead, there was a quiet satisfaction at the idea that Bellona would experience a degree happiness as an outcome of her time on Ledan, something that had always been a rare quality in her life.

They also found some amusement in the location she had chosen for her seduction. Defiance had always been part of her personality.

Then their gaze fell upon Reynard Cardenas, who still stood in his warm corner, holding sway upon the gathered family. Of everyone in the room, his was the loudest voice. He rarely bothered to modulate. There was no need—everyone was eager to hear what he said…if they were wise.

Sang realized they felt dismay, after all. Not everyone in the family would be pleased by the man in Bellona's arms.

Chapter Eight

Cardenas (Findlay IV), Findlay System, Eriuman Republic.

It took five weeks for the family to erupt over Khalil Ready, which was completely unsurprising to Sang. There could be no immediate or direct protest about her relationship as Eriuman women were technically free to choose their partners.

Before their venture into the heart of Karassian lands, Sang had found the subjective reality of Eriuman affairs of the heart perfectly natural. Now, though, they had a different perspective to measure it by. So did Bellona, who carried all her memories of Xenia's pleasant life in Ledan.

In this matter, Karassians had a more open approach. Alliances, dalliances, contracts, marriages, it was all of utter disinterest to Karassians, unless a relationship soured, or was settled for the long term, or provided some other drama they could watch from afar. The 'who' was less important than the 'how'.

Eriumans, though, cared deeply about the couplings of their family members, especially if breeding was involved. Then, family manipulations to arrange the "right" partner emerged in force. The longer a seemingly casual and unsuitable alliance continued, the stronger the family response to it.

Max was the first to speak to Bellona directly about Khalil. Sang suspected the indelicate directness was a result of his military life, which demanded he return to service, forcing him to speak.

Sang spent the morning gathering Max's possessions and stowing them in the carryall for return to the *Decimus*, while listening for Bellona's return. She and Khalil had hiked to the peak of the hill the homebase was located upon. It was a four hour journey both ways and the better part of a day, if one lingered at the lonely peak. There was a hot spring just below the peak that would beckon the pair, too.

Max dithered impatiently, picking up and putting down childhood possessions that were kept on the shelf by his big desk. He sat, then stood, then sat again.

"The satellite has them nearly back to the house," Sang observed, after consulting with the house AI. "They are making better time on the lower slopes, too."

Max nodded, pretending only a mild interest.

As it was close to both Max's departure time and the early evening partake, Sang went to the kitchens and arranged for Max a meal of several hundred calories—enough to keep his energy up and his mood stable. Max fell on the hotpot and pie with a grunt of approval and devoured it quickly.

By the time he was done, Sang could hear Bellona's voice from the front of the house, as she spoke to someone there. She sounded happy.

Max jumped up, shoving the plates away. "Come with me," he told Sang.

Sang followed him out to the public rooms.

Max caught up with Bellona in the gallery, the wide and even longer hall that gave access to the private suites. Like the gathering room, the gallery had no solid walls on either side, just fields to keep the inclement weather out. Today, the fields were down. The late afternoon air was just turning from warm to cool.

Max beckoned Bellona over. Khalil stayed by the other side of the gallery and looked out at the lengthening shadows.

"You're wearing your uniform," Bellona told Max.

"I've been called back. There's an offensive…well, you don't need the details."

"An offensive where?"

"It doesn't matter. I don't have time, anyway. I'm already dangerously close to being late."

Bellona frowned. "There was something I wanted to talk to you about. I haven't had a chance, lately."

Max's gaze flickered toward Khalil. "Understandable," he said heavily. "That's what I wanted to talk to you about."

Bellona's face closed over. Her jaw flexed, as anger flickered in her eyes.

Max read her reaction as easily as Sang had. He shook his head. "Put your claws back, Bellona. You know I don't care about who you're with. You must stop flaunting in him front of Father, though."

"Why?" she demanded.

"You think I don't know you're doing it deliberately? You know that every time he sees you with Khalil, it gnaws him. You think that Father doesn't know you're baiting him, too?"

Bellona crossed her arms. She looked very young, with the fresh glow of exertion on her face, but the defiance had gone. Now she merely looked thoughtful. "I might have known that if he had only spoken to me about more than the weather, lately."

"Those are not conversations that come easily to him. You know what he's like, Bellona. Do you really want to force Father to speak to you over something like this? It won't end happily."

"That's where you're wrong," Bellona said, her voice smooth and strong. Confident. "I don't play by family rules anymore. The delicate stepping around in circles. The prevarications. All of it. I'm done, Max."

"Not while you're living here, you are not."

"I can't live anywhere else," she said bitterly. "Not anymore. Maybe I never could, despite trying. Why *did* you take me off the planet? Why was I on the *Hathaway*?"

Max grew still. He rubbed the back of his neck. "I think it's a good thing you can't remember."

"If I did remember, would I still be here?" Bellona asked. "Would I *want* to be here?"

Sang looked at Max, as interested in the answer as Bellona.

Max swallowed. "I don't know."

"You don't know, or you won't tell me?"

"You wouldn't tell *me!*" Max shot back. "You came to me, more upset than I've ever seen you in my life. You were verging on hysterical and you wouldn't say what was wrong. You just begged me to get you away, far away."

Khalil had stopped pretending to be interested in the view. He stood with his legs spread and his hands at the ready, watching the siblings.

Bellona stared at Max. "What *happened*?" she muttered.

Max retreated to the practical. "Have you tried to restore the memory? Bots? Hypnosis?"

Bellona rolled her eyes impatiently.

Max nodded. "Then maybe you should stop digging at it. Either it will come back, or it won't. Either way, I don't think you'll like it when it does. You were not yourself that night, Bell."

Bellona shifted on her feet. The boots and trousers she favored these days vexed her mother, but Sang thought they suited her. She scowled. "I haven't been myself for a very long time," she said, her voice harsh. "One more ripple won't be noticed amongst the churn."

Sang cleared their throat. "The time..." they murmured, as their sense of passing time was always more accurate than most humans and far more accurate than Max's.

Max nodded. "I have to go. I can't keep the shuttle waiting." He gripped Bellona's arms and gave her a shake. "You take care of yourself."

"Always," she said easily.

"I mean it."

"I will."

Max looked at Sang. "I want you to watch out for her, Sang."

Sang nodded.

"I don't need a help-meet," Bellona protested.

"You're about to lose one of your few allies in the family," Max said gravely. "I'm compensating for that as much as I can. Let Sang help. They're very good at it."

"They are," Khalil said quietly, from his observer's place across the gallery.

Bellona sighed. "Very well."

Max hugged her. It was an impulsive movement and Bellona stood with her arms stiffly at her sides, caught by surprise.

Max glanced at Khalil and nodded, then stepped around Bellona and strode down the gallery, heading for the front of the house, where he would find Reynard and Iulia and say his goodbyes.

Sang saw the temper simmering in Bellona's face as she studied them. The resentment was unmistakable. "We will see Max off," they said.

"Good idea," she said shortly.

#

For a week after Max's departure, a lull held the family. Bellona did her best to ignore Sang, although her disregard was not aimed purely at Sang. She ignored everyone, including her father. She and Khalil toured the city, hiked a lot and spent time in the movement suite with the doors sealed, from where the sound of clashing weapons could be heard. Bellona was training Khalil more effectively than Sang could. Sang's coaching became a supplement, instead, rounding out Khalil's skills.

"It helps her keep the memories fresh," Khalil confessed to Sang after a long session from which he emerged sweating and exhausted. "It reminds her of who she was."

"She wishes to remember being Xenia?"

"The Xenia she remembers was happy. She had friends. A life that was content. It doesn't matter that it was all an illusion. It felt real enough when she was living it." Khalil frowned. "And it helps her ignore the news."

The war news was not good. Part of Sang's function was to collate news and present it daily. When Max was not there, Sang merely collected. They did not know how Bellona was acquiring her news updates, for she did not ask Sang for them. Perhaps it had not occurred to her that Sang could provide the service. Iulia, as head of the family, was the only woman assigned a personal assistant. Bellona had grown up without one, as most women in minor positions in Eriuman households did. It was considered a waste to provide each of them with an assistant, so Bellona had never learned to work with one.

The terminal in Bellona's private suite was smart enough to build a daily update, although it was not an AI and would not adapt the feed to suit her waxing and waning interests. It didn't matter for right now, because all the news was negative. Lost ships, with all hands. Lost territories, which Erium found almost more painful than the loss of lives. While losses were an accepted part of war, it was the manner of the more recent losses that grated. The Karassians had taken Max's innovations with smaller, personal fighting craft and applied it with the usual Karassian slap-dash passion and drive. The little fighters they were using against Eriuman cruisers had been too quickly designed and were inclined to explode upon launch or even in mid-flight. They often broke down. Yet, when they were working, they were *fast* and they were lethal. Max's tactic of overwhelming Karassian cruisers with Eriuman fighter craft, the constant barrage bringing them to their knees, was being used against the Eriuman Navy now.

So the silence and stillness lasted for a week after Max's departure, while Iulia stayed in her rooms and Bellona and Khalil roamed the city for long hours each day.

Then Reynard announced a formal dinner party, to which Khalil was *not* invited.

Bellona summoned Sang to her suite and showed them the invitation on her screen.

"Oh, that is…awkward," Sang decided. "It is a direct shot

across the bows, too."

Bellona nodded. "Formal dinner parties are never odd-numbered. They'll have someone there. Who? Would they dare push my cousin Delben at me again?"

Sang smiled. "Delben is married these days, with six children."

"He was heartbroken by my disappearance, clearly."

Sang considered the invitation. "It is a formal invitation to which you must respond. You could simply not attend."

"Decline, or accept and fail to show?" Bellona grimaced. "Either is…gutless."

"Under the circumstances, it could be argued as the prudent move."

"Whose side are you on, Sang?" she asked. "You're a family member, too."

"Max asked us to watch out for you."

"This falls under 'watching out'?"

"I am a generalist assistant," Sang pointed out. "My parameters range as far as my experience tells me they need to."

"Like buying a luxury Karassian yacht to smuggle me off Kachmar?" Bellona asked. She was still smiling. "Khalil told me."

"That is a very good example."

"If your parameters are so flexible, then you can help me with this." She pointed at the screen again.

"You intend to go?"

"Only to learn how serious my father is about pushing

the family agenda on me. If I can't take Khalil, I want you there."

"It would be inappropriate for us to sit at a table that has no formal place laid for us."

"You can stand next to Riz and Wait if that makes you feel better. I want you there in formals, though. I want it known you're with me. And I want you to observe everything that happens so I can analyze it later."

"We would be most happy to help you with this."

Bellona's smile returned in full force. "I also want you to make me a dress. Khalil says you're skilled at design."

"It is a matter of mathematics, that is all."

"Esthetics have something to do with it. Can you make me a dress that will tell everyone there I don't care?"

"Is that the message you wish to send?"

Bellona frowned. "Yes."

"Then we know exactly what you should wear."

#

Sang made the preparations carefully. Their first step was to consult with Khalil, who approved the plan wholeheartedly. "Bellona is right. You need to be there, if I cannot be. No one sees you."

"They will, this time," Sang pointed out.

"They might for a few seconds, but they've had a lifetime of ignoring you. They'll soon forget you're there, once the surprise has worn off."

On the evening of the party, Sang presented themselves to Bellona. Khalil, sitting in the easy chair he favored, smiled. "Impressive, Sang."

Bellona walked all around them. "Yes, it is," she decided. "Male, tonight, Sang?"

Sang looked down at the dark formal trousers and jacket. "It is appropriate we favor the male gender tonight if you wish to impart the maximum impact."

Khalil pointed to the terminal where an Eriuman profile rotated. "If they have invited this Captain Ahn Delucas that Sang has decided is the one, then Sang is right. A sharp jab at his competitive nature will have him reacting without filters. There are rumors he likes to deal with opposition without witnesses, though."

"That won't be an issue tonight," Bellona said. She held her hands out from her sides. "How do I look?"

Sang considered the scuffed boots, the rumpled black trousers and the even more disreputable shirt. Her hair was loose, as usual and ringlets hung about her face in delightful disorder. She wore no makeup and no jewelry.

"They will know exactly how little you care, except that you will be standing next to Sang, whose appearance disputes that," Khalil decided.

"Only for those who notice Sang at all," Bellona said. "My father will get the message, though." She gripped Sang's elbow. "Let's go."

Eleven people stood in the gathering room, each holding

a cup, when Sang and Bellona walked into the room. Sang catalogued reactions as Bellona had requested. Most of the guests were slow to notice their entry, because they were concentrating on their own conversations—especially those surrounding Reynard. There were some puzzled expressions and some amused ones. Lips parted. Eyes widened.

The man standing next to Reynard was a stranger, yet Sang knew the face. Captain Ahn Delucas, wearing the full uniform of the Eriuman Navy.

Iulia stepped around the group she had been a part of and hurried over to where Bellona and Sang stood by the inner doorway. She trailed silk, lace and perfume. Her eyes were narrowed, while her face was held in a stiff neutral expression. "Are you mad?" she whispered. "Go back to your rooms and change into something more suitable, as quickly as you can. This needn't be a disaster. I will tell your father you were running so late, you thought it wise to appear first, then dress properly. Go. Go!" She pushed at Bellona's shoulder, trying to turn her and get her out of the room.

"I'm as dressed as I will get, Mother," Bellona said. "I am comfortable and tidy."

"You cannot represent the family looking as you do," Iulia hissed back. There was a tic at the corner of her eye, fluttering quickly.

"I don't remember being asked to do that."

Iulia's tic increased. "You're not a fool. Neither am I. You know very well these events are a showcase for the family."

Gaubert came up to them. The clean, square line of the jaw that was a family trait was softer on him, blurred by good living and an easy acceptance of his status. He touched Bellona's shoulder. "You are looking casual, niece."

"I am, thank you," Bellona shot back. "Sang, a drink, please."

"No," Iulia snapped. "She is returning to her room."

Sang looked at Bellona. She stared right back.

Instead of leaving her with her mother and uncle, Sang raised their hand and beckoned one of the help-meets over. Sang smiled their thanks and took two of the cups from the tray they were carrying and handed Bellona one of them.

Gaubert watched Sang, a smile forming and growing broader. "How quaint," he murmured and drank deeply from his own cup.

Iulia gripped Bellona's forearm as she tried to lift the cup to her mouth. "No," she said, her voice low and hard. "Hear me. Stop this at once, Bellona. You will gain nothing from defying your father in this way."

Bellona swayed to one side, to look around Iulia's shoulder. She smiled. "I have already gained everything I intended."

Sang looked in the direction Bellona had glanced. Reynard was standing near the big dinner table, talking to Delucas. His face was dark with suppressed anger. As Sang looked, Reynard's gaze flicked toward Bellona.

Bellona shook off her mother's grip and sipped from the

cup. "Toss me out, mother," she said. "Please. You'll be doing me a favor."

Gaubert tisked in delighted disapproval. He was enjoying the moment.

Iulia dropped her hand. "Sending you away will only call more attention to your waywardness. We will brazen this out. Sang, take your post."

Sang looked at Bellona for direction. She nodded. "Yes, I think my point has been made," she said softly. "Thank you, Sang. I will not divide your loyalty any more tonight."

Sang felt a need to contradict her observation and held it back, for it would not contribute to the play they were helping perform right now. Instead, Sang nodded and moved over to where Riz and Wait stood, in the darker corner of the room. As they went, they sipped the wine, then added the cup to the return tray. They presumed no one would notice the audacious act, except Riz and Wait, who both looked shocked.

Iulia pulled Bellona over to where her father was standing, her knuckles white where she gripped Bellona's arm. Delucas turned to face the approaching women, a pleasant smile stitched on his flat face.

Sang focused their hearing.

Reynard's grip on his cup tightened, as he said in a jovial tone; "Captain, I present to you my daughter, Bellona Cardenas Scordina de Deluca. Bellona, I recommend to you Captain Ahn Delucas Scordino de Carosa."

Ahn inclined his head. "It is a great pleasure, Bellona, to finally meet you. You have been much in the news lately."

It was now Bellona's turn to express her appreciation for his company and add a light compliment of some sort. Sang had seen the pattern repeated thousands of times.

Bellona drained her cup and put it on the table by her hip, disturbing the neatly laid pattern of plates and utensils. "Your ship is the *Livius*, yes, Captain?"

Ahn's pleasant expression faded. "Indeed," he said, his tone flat.

"A dreadnought of the third generation," Bellona added. "Tell me, what strategies have you developed to counter the Karassian single-man fighters?"

Reynard cleared his throat. "This is barely a fit discussion for here and now."

"I guarantee it is the only subject Captain Delucas thinks about these days," Bellona said, staring at Ahn.

Ahn's smile this time looked as though it was pulled from him without his permission. "You are very perceptive," he said shortly.

Iulia sighed. "Oh dear…"

"Really, Captain, I would like to hear your thoughts about this," Bellona added. "It seems to me that my brother's idea to carry lightweight fighters gave the Eriuman Navy a short advantage that has now been completely neutralized by the Karassian imitations. Instead, you're having to deal with a problem of your own making."

"You would be right," Ahn said, his attention thoroughly caught.

"An impasse," Bellona said.

"Indeed."

"However, could you not also argue that the entire undeclared war, going back to the destruction of the *Valerianus*, has been on the whole a search for a way to break the impasse?"

Ahn nodded. "A constant impasse, yes. As soon as we or the Karassians discover a weakness to exploit, the other side imitates that strategy."

"Then both sides adapt and you're back to the impasse," Bellona added.

Anh drew in a slow, deep breath. "You have an unusual clarity of thinking."

"It comes from having lived in both worlds," she said shortly.

Anh drew back. He clearly did not appreciate the reminder of her recent history.

Iulia leapt to minimize the damage. "I am desperately hungry. Reynard, may we start the meal?"

"That would be appropriate," Reynard said slowly, as if his mind was far away. He was staring at Bellona and Sang suspected that for the first time in his long life, Reynard Cardenas was seeing his daughter without filters.

Sang motioned to the help-meets, who hurried to withdraw chairs from the table and help the guests seat themselves. Ahn Delucas was seated next to Bellona. Sang placed themselves directly behind her chair and enjoyed the startled look Iulia gave them.

Unlike most formal dinners that Sang had attended, this one held the promise of novelty.

Chapter Nine

Cardenas (Findlay IV), Findlay System, Eriuman Republic.

After ninety minutes of grappling drills under the intense sun of midday, both Khalil and Sang were happy to lie on the lawn for a moment and recover.

Sang listened to the hum of insects, Khalil's heavy breath and the whisper of a breeze in the tops of the trees nearby. Here in the heart of the family garden, not a hint of the city that lay all around disturbed the peace. Nothing could be glimpsed through the bordering trees and bushes.

This was Max's favorite section of the sprawling gardens. It was where he had taken most of his combat training and Sang had spent long hours standing at the narrow entrance, watching the sessions.

It had seemed appropriate to bring Khalil here when Sang had found him pacing the gallery. The man had been angry and miserable. "She will not stir from the bed," he said. "She will not speak to me. To *me*." His distress was plain. "What happened last night?"

Sang had suggested the training session as an excuse to get them both out of the house and into a location where they could speak freely, yet Sang had found the exertion a welcome relief. They only wished they had anticipated the activity and worn something lighter. Today was one of the early, hot days that heralded the coming of summer. Sang plucked the shirt away from their chest.

Khalil grunted, watching the movement. Then he sat up and pulled the tunic over his head and tossed it away. "Better," he decided, rotating his bare shoulders.

"One often does not get to choose what clothes to wear in a battle. The battle arrives unannounced, in a location and time that is usually highly inconvenient," Sang said, remembering the ex-Navy instructor bawling that fact at Max and Bellona, while they fought to stay awake and train in the small hours of the night, both wearing nothing more than the lightest of sleepwear and robes.

"So I should wear combat gear at all times?" Khalil asked, sounding both tired and amused.

"Do you feel you might be called upon to fight at any instant?" Sang asked.

Khalil propped himself up on his arms. "Here, I always feel that way." He met Sang's gaze. "What happened last night?"

Sang cast their mind back to the previous evening. The dinner party had proceeded choppily, with Bellona keeping Anh Delucas on his toes with pointed questions and observations, while Reynard and Iulia did their best to redirect the conversation whenever they could. The remaining dinner guests, all close relatives of Reynard's, had tried to follow their hosts' leads, hiding their discomfort at the raw subjects Bellona raised—abduction, annexation, hostages, slavery, subjugation, death ratios, acceptable loss rates, AI mortality priorities... Sang suspected that few of the guests had ever openly discussed such matters even in the privacy of their own homes, let alone over a formal dinner table.

"Bellona talked to Captain Ahn," Sang told Khalil. "To speak to him was exactly what Reynard and Iulia wanted, only not at all the outcome they expected. Ahn found Bellona fascinating...and uncomfortable."

Khalil smiled. "She can have that effect, if one forgets her experience."

"We believe all her family would prefer to forget Ledan ever happened. Bellona reminded them, last night. It was a masterful display of expertise in a subject that Eriumans rarely speak about openly." Sang shifted on the lawn, looking for a more comfortable position on the soft gray tufts.

Khalil waited.

Sang sighed. "It happened when dessert was served."

"*What* happened?" Khalil coaxed.

"We are not entirely certain. Bellona bent to sniff the bowl in front of her." Sang frowned. They had reviewed the sequence many times since it had happened. She had bent to sniff the concoction, a warm treat redolent with spices. Many of the other guests were doing the same and sighing with pleasure.

Bellona, though, had frozen, her gaze on the dish and her hand gripping the edge of the table. A frantic pulse throbbed at the base of her neck.

Sang noticed her distress quickly. Instantly, they turned to the sideboard, picked up one of the extra dishes and scooped up a mouthful of the dessert, analyzing it for poisons, toxins and histamines.

The explosion of spice flavors was pleasant, but in no way was it alarming. The dessert was completely innocent. Not even the scent it gave off was harmful.

Other guests were noticing her reaction. Anh put down his spoon and touched her arm. "Bellona?" he asked quietly, leaning closer so others would not hear the soft enquiry.

Sang leaned between them. "Excuse me, Captain," they told Ahn and picked up the bowl in front of Bellona and sampled it. It was identical.

Sang bent to examine Bellona. Perspiration dotted her temples. She breathed raggedly through parted lips. Her eyes were still fixed on the place where the bowl had been sitting, unblinking. The pupils were very large.

Carefully, they laid their hand on her shoulder and gave her a gentle shake. "Bellona."

She drew in a rushed, deep breath and stirred, bringing her hand to her head. "I...have to go." She lurched from the table, brushing past Gaubert, who sat on her left, ignoring the hand he raised to help her.

"Sang," Iulia said shortly, in a tone Sang understood.

They caught up with Bellona and assisted her from the room, guiding her in a straighter line than the weaving path she had been following.

Bellona shuddered as they walked. "I could almost see it," she murmured, her voice thick.

"See what?" Sang asked.

"I don't know! I can't remember."

Sang paused outside the entrance to her suite of rooms, to give her a chance to deny them entry if she wished, as Khalil was in there.

Bellona put her hand on the door, propping herself up. "I feel...sick."

"Should we assist you? An anti-nausea shot, perhaps..."

Bellona shook her head, then held still and pressed her fingers to her temple once more. "No. No cures. No remedies. I need to find out." She touched the doorplate and moved out of the way as the door swung open. She met Sang's eyes. "Thank you," she said simply. "I will be fine now."

Sang understood why she was lying. "It got you out of the dinner party," they pointed out, trying to lift the mood.

Her smile was barely there, yet it *was* a smile. "Yes, I planned it all along. A way to avoid the after-dinner wine on the terrace that Anh would undoubtedly have suggested. Good night, Sang."

Sang watched until the door was closed and sealed once more, then moved through the mostly silent house to their own small quarters. There was no point in returning to the dinner party. Their presence would act as a reminder to everyone and they did not enjoy being resented.

When they had finished relating the event to Khalil, he remained silent for a long moment. There were very few people who were as comfortable with silences as Khalil was.

"She said 'I could almost see it'?"

"Yes."

Again, the deep silence. Then Khalil sat up, taking the weight off his arms. He brushed the grass off his palms. "I remember the land where I lived as a child. The sun was more orange than this one—I found out later it was just barely within the livable zone and only the equatorial areas of my world were sustaining, but those areas were warm and comfortable. I don't remember harsh winters, of course. Just endless warm days. The earth was a deep, dark brown, darker than any earth I have seen since. The sky was nearly always cloudless. I would walk for hours and hours, watching the way the mountains never seemed to come any closer. They were so tall. Even now, I have never seen taller mountains. They towered over us who lived in that tiny village. They surrounded the city, a day's ride away. The mountains looked after me, I thought, for they were everywhere I went. I remember those days with a fondness that makes me smile. I was innocent. I knew nothing of the greater world beyond provincial space."

"Most children are so," Sang said in agreement, wondering why Khalil was telling them this. As he had never spoken about his life before meeting Bellona, Sang did not interrupt him now. Later, they would analyze every word for implications, assumptions that could be made and hidden facts. It was a natural function to gather data about those surrounding the one they worked for, especially those who were in her bed.

Khalil pointed with his freshly brushed-off hand. "There is a plant over there—I have no idea what it is, yet when I get near it, I can smell it. It is an aroma very close to the one given off by the bushes the farm directors planted alongside their crops to ward off birds. When I smell that plant, Sang, I don't just remember the mountains and the earth with simple fondness. For a moment, it is as if I am actually there. I can recall details that I have long forgotten. The way the earth squeezed through my toes when I ran through freshly ploughed fields. The sun on my face. The cold air that came off the peaks when the wind was right, with the smell of snow riding on them. The tartness of the berries from those bushes...my mouth watered when I recalled it."

Sang considered that. "A repressed memory," they said. "Did the spice force her to recall a memory of Xenia? The fighter, not the dancer?"

Khalil shook his head. "Those memories are not suppressed. They're not there at all. There is only one memory I know of that Bellona cannot recall even when she tries."

"Why she left Cardenas," Sang concluded.

Khalil was staring at the plant that had evoked his childhood.

"Should we arrange for a miniature to be created for you?" Sang asked.

Khalil shuddered, his smile fading. "No, thank you." He brushed his hands off once more, even though they were clean. "Not every memory of home is a pleasant one. The rest...can remain just memories. I do not care to repeat them."

Sang tried to sort through the courses of action that lay open to them now that Khalil had proposed this enticing possibility. How could they help Bellona retrieve the memory? *Should* they? Perhaps, like Khalil's past, it was a memory best left buried.

"Have you ever wondered what goes into the making of a hero, Sang?"

Sang frowned. "I have not studied heroes at all, although the Eriuman Navy decorates many of them every year."

Khalil laughed. "I mean, a *real* hero. A leader, a visionary, someone who emerges from obscurity to blazing glory, changing the world with their deeds. True heroes, Sang, are rare. They burst upon the known worlds once every thousand generations or more and they leave a mark that is never forgotten."

"Mia Rasmussen," Sang suggested.

"Svend Murat Kovac," Khalil added. "Ben the Glorious. The Emperor of Xylander."

"Dusan Funard."

"Susan the Savior," Khalil said. "See, the names come very easily to you. To everyone. Their names are never forgotten. Their impact upon the known worlds is endless and immeasurable. Think of how different life would be if Dusan Funard had not fought every cynic and politician in his way and made the first null engine, two thousand years ago."

Sang catalogued all he knew of the people they had swiftly named. "Many of them come from humble beginnings and dire circumstances," Sang pointed out. "Do you feel your own unfortunate experiences qualify you as a potential hero?"

This time Khalil's laughter came from deep in his belly. He shook with it and wiped away tears, as paroxysms swept over him. When he had himself under control once more, he sighed and wiped at his eyes one last time. "You're smart, Sang. No argument. When you say things like that, though, I am reminded that you are not altogether human."

Sang felt no offense. "We are always willing to learn."

"I'm not a hero," Khalil said. "I can never be one. I don't *want* to be one."

"Yet you study them."

"I do."

"Why?"

He shrugged. "Curiosity, I suppose. If the human chaos throws up a hero every thousand generations or so, we are long overdue for a hero of our times. I often wonder what that hero might look like and how they will change the known worlds."

"You do not like the known worlds as they are?"

"Does anyone?"

Sang considered the question seriously. "We would not exist in different circumstances, so we are grateful for these circumstances. Other than that, they are what they are."

"Bellona is troubling you, too, isn't she?"

Sang sighed. "Max was specific in the responsibilities he assigned us. While Bellona is…suffering, we are not abiding by that assignment. Yet, the way ahead is not clear. Perhaps it is better she live with the frustration of a lost memory, than unearth a memory that…"

"Changes everything?" Khalil asked.

"Yes. Which means we must live with failure. That is not a comfortable thought for one such as we, who prefers binary decisions."

"Humans have been dealing with such dilemmas throughout history."

Sang nodded. "We are aware of that. We even tried writing down our thought processes as the exercise seems to provide clarity to others." Sang shrugged. "Yet, the dilemma remains."

"How, exactly, did you try writing down your thoughts?" Khalil asked curiously.

"The usual way. We spoke aloud while the archivist recorded."

Khalil smiled. "Give me an example. Recite something you wrote."

Puzzled, Sang recalled the writing session. Because of their perfect recall, the act of writing and storing thoughts was doubly useless. Nevertheless, Sang selected an innocuous phrase. *"We struggle to understand how we might better —"*

"That's why it didn't work for you," Khalil said, interrupting.

Sang frowned.

"We this. *We* that. No group in history has ever been able to group-think a solution better or faster than a clear-thinking individual — and you are that, Sang."

"Clear thinking?"

"Transparently clear." Khalil patted their shoulder. "Try again." He got to his feet. "Time to beat your skinny frame into submission. Get up."

#

Much later that night, when Sang had assured themselves that Bellona rested comfortably, even if her thoughts were plaguing her, and long after the house had grown still and dark, Sang directed the house AI to extrude recording sheets and print a stylus keyed to the sheets.

Trembling with their own daring, Sang sat at the small table, the stylus hovering over the blank sheet. They had learned rudimentary writing skills as part of their forced development while still emerging from the growth tanks, so the act of writing was not completely foreign to them. The skill was sometimes required as a form of record-keeping. Such records were always converted to more permanent states, later.

Sang wrote.

Khalil thinks we are troubled about Bellona's state of mind.

Sang read the crude letters aloud, then glanced around. There was no one to hear.

They scratched out the sentence. There was an intimate secrecy about the act of writing, especially on record sheets that no one could access through a terminal, or recall upon a screen somewhere else. Not even the absolutely discreet household archivist held the words inside it. They were for Sang alone.

That gave them the courage to write again, the letters already forming faster.

We are troubled about Bellona's state of mind.

Sang read the sentence. It had no impact. They drew a hard line through it and gripped the stylus, hovering once more. Then, with a sucked-in breath, they wrote quickly, before they could change their minds. They dropped the stylus and sat back to study the single short line they had written.

I am afraid for Bellona.

"Truth," Sang whispered, then covered their eyes and wept.

Chapter Ten

Cardenas (Findlay IV), Findlay System, Eriuman Republic.

Bellona seemed to return to her normal spirits the next day, although Sang often caught her staring at nothing, her focus turned inward, as she searched memories. Sang could not discourage her from the practice. All they could do was monitor — and worry.

As was the family practice with uncomfortable subjects, the events at the dinner party went unremarked. It was as if they had not happened. Sang considered that a reprieve.

Ten days after the dinner party, Bellona sent for Sang and ordered them to sit. "Witness mode, Sang," she said, which forced Sang to remain silent, in a purely observation mode. They noted that the household aide designated "Dani" stood by Bellona's divan. Its metal face was devoid of emotion.

Khalil came in wearing a frown. "The terminal in the gallery said you were looking for me." He spent a lot of time sitting against the sun-warmed pillars there. Thinking, he said, and watching the sun on the grass.

Bellona turned from her pacing. "Dani, repeat the report back, please."

Dani opened its mouth. "Secure Document Seven Eight Six Dash Em Three, from Archive Four Six Three, extracted from Bureau Datahouse Gamma, seal intact. Subject—"

"Stop," Bellona ordered. She looked at Khalil. "Do you know what the subject is?"

Khalil's gaze was on Dani. "About me, I imagine," he said. His voice was remote.

"Yes," Bellona said flatly. "This is a *Bureau* record!"

Khalil looked at her. "Use the proper name, if you must use it at all. The Wyan Oushxiu, Generation 98, of Marijus Prime."

"I don't care!" Bellona raged. "You're one of the Bureau. A human computer freak."

Khalil's gaze shifted to Sang.

"Sang can't talk. They're in witness mode."

Khalil's shoulders fell. "You think you need a witness? With me?" The pain in his voice was vivid.

"I don't know what to think," Bellona shot back. "Is it true?" Then she laughed. It was a raw sound. "What am I asking? That's a bonded, sealed document, straight out of the Bureau's own archives on Marijus. Its authenticity is beyond dispute. It says you are a member of the Bureau, that you have been all along…" She swallowed. "Even before Ledan."

Khalil looked at Dani once more. His expression was indecipherable, but bitterness was part of it. "The Bureau are not human computers," he said, his voice low. "They *use* digital intelligence. They build it. Vast artificial minds with a power well beyond our human ability to think and process. Why does everyone not understand that? The Bureau does not hide the fact."

"They just steal babies and seal them in with a terminal and they grow up knowing nothing about humans. They *think* they're computers!"

Khalil shook his head, his expression sad. "They recruit older children, when they show the type of thinking that allows a human to interface with advanced digital minds. They become interpreters. Researchers."

Bellona breathed heavily, stress taxing her. "The Bureau twists history, to serve its own ends." It was a common belief.

Khalil sighed. "They predict, that is all, based upon statistical renderings of history. They are wrong as often as they are right."

Sang made a notation. In fact, the Bureau was right far more often than it was wrong. Businesses and corporations across the known worlds used Bureau predictions to set their policies and directions, while both the Homogeny and the Republic leveraged predictions for an advantage in the war. Everyone used Bureau computers to run their lives, no matter who they were or where their allegiance lay. To use anything else was to risk losing data, functionality, time and money.

"Of course you defend them," Bellona said. "You're one of them."

"Not anymore."

For the first time, Bellona looked surprised. Her fury checked. "How can that be? Who *do* you answer to, if not them?"

"Since Ledan?" he asked. "No one." He pointed at Dani. "Did you ask for the date stamp, when you were reviewing the file? How old is it?"

Doubt shadowed her face. "You *were* Bureau…"

Khalil rubbed the back of his neck, ruffling the shorn locks there. "Yes, but —"

"I don't care about justifications and excuses. You lied to me."

"Everyone has secrets, Bellona."

"Affairs and trivialities! You knew yours would make a difference. That's why you didn't tell me."

"I didn't tell you because it was no longer relevant…and yes, I was afraid that if I did, you would treat me differently. One gets very tired of being looked at as if they are some sort of monster, or worse, not being seen at all." There was bitterness in his voice.

Sang could not react. Instead, they made a notation.

"Do you know how many worlds, how many cities, the countless corporations I have dealt with, Bellona? All of them saw me as a means to an end. The great computing genius of the Bureau at their disposal, working for them, providing miraculous, life-changing answers for them!" He threw out his hand. "*You* didn't look at me that way."

"On Ledan, when I didn't know who you were," Bellona

said flatly.

"You *did* know!" His frustration made him shift on his feet. "Review your memories! I was Ari, but I was Bureau, there to rebuild computers. You didn't care."

Bellona swallowed. "Why did I not remember that?" Her anger was diminishing.

"None of your memories from then have any strong emotion. They don't recur because there is nothing to remind you of them."

"Then how is it you remember them?"

"Because *you* were there!"

Bellona whirled away, a sharp movement, putting her back to him. "You told me you were from a free state."

"You think the Bureau only recruits Karassians and Eriumans?" Khalil asked. "I was on Atticus. I was eleven and I was alone. They offered comfort and shelter and a better education than I was getting from the homeless there. I took their offer, Bellona, even though they did not hide that they were Bureau."

Sang made another notation. The world that Khalil had described, the one that the scent of a plant had evoked, had looked nothing like the industrial complexes of Atticus...and Khalil had not been alone in that place. There had been family there, too. No one with leisure and health to roam the fields and stare at the mountains was without loved ones.

Bellona did not move. She did not react. Sang could not see her face, either.

"I understand digital minds, Bellona," Khalil said. "That's why they took me. The vast power at the Bureau's disposal, the huge minds—they need...friends. Guidance. Especially when they're young. Then the Bureau realized I was as comfortable dealing with humans as I was with computers and I became a field agent, providing a human face for their biggest transactions."

"A salesman?" Bellona asked. Her tone was one of disinterest.

"A representative. You have to understand, Bellona. Some of the humans that the Bureau recruit really *are* freaks. They can no more interface with human society than the intelligences they build. Yet *I* can. I still look human."

Bellona turned then, startled. Sang made another notation, for later consideration. "Then they *are* monsters."

"Monsters are something to be afraid of. You would not be afraid of the Bureau's oldest humans, if you were permitted to see them. They would be pitiable, if they thought themselves unfortunate, only they do not. They are happy, even though most of them can no longer walk because their legs have atrophied. They are isolated and difficult to understand because they rarely use human speech. Within the Bureau they have an acceptance they could find nowhere else."

"That is where you will end up?" Bellona asked, horror in her eyes.

"I am not an interpreter," Khalil said. "I never would have been. Now, I am not even a member of the Bureau."

Bellona considered that. "Why did you leave?"

"Because of you."

She shook her head. "You would not voluntarily leave that which gave you meaning."

"Unless I found meaning somewhere else."

"Then why not tell me who you really were?"

"Because I wasn't that man anymore."

"Pedantry!"

"You want truth, Bellona? You won't like it."

"I would rather hate you for your true qualities than hate the mask you hold up."

Khalil closed his eyes, absorbing it. "Very well," he said softly. He sighed and opened his eyes once more. In recording mode as they were, Sang found it all too easy to decipher the defeat in the angle of his shoulders. Khalil knew he had lost everything. "At least, let Sang be themselves," he said softly. "That robotic stare is unsettling. Sang will still remember everything later."

"You would prefer no formal record, then," Bellona surmised.

"Not for this," he said flatly.

Bellona looked at Sang. "End witness mode," she told them.

Sang breathed deeply, blinking. "Thank you."

Bellona looked at Khalil. "Speak," she said coldly.

Instead, he walked about in a tight circle, building himself to it.

"Know that nothing you say will restore my faith in you, Khalil Ready," Bellona added. "All you can do now is redeem your character, if you can."

He nodded. "I will be content with that. The words are difficult, though. Outsiders do not understand that world, the life."

"Try," she urged him.

"I was a field agent. That means more than it appears. For the inner levels of the Bureau, *everything* has to be brokered — the acquisition of human food, the purchase of raw materials for building components, arranging housekeeping, medical care, even something as simple as clothing had to be arranged via someone like me, who could move about in the world and deal with humans. I have been given tasks in my time that seemed puny and meaningless, until I remembered that the task-giver was incapable of completing it for themselves."

Sang remembered the water and the cloth that had been left for them.

"You were assigned to follow me?" Bellona demanded.

"I was told to assess a potential hero."

Sang felt as though they were gawping just as Bellona was.

Khalil sighed again. "The Bureau has known for more than ten years that a war is coming. A real one, not this informal slap exchange between the Homogeny and the Republic. A war that will draw in everyone in the known worlds, that will change the direction of life itself. When the neural mind declared the coming of the war, the Bureau set themselves the tasks of finding the hero that the war would produce."

Bellona shook her head. "Heroes aren't made just by wars."

"They are made by pressure, which wars provide. Overwhelming pressure provokes extreme response and the right response, for the right reasons, creates a hero. Such a hero can effect great change, especially for those who follow him."

Bellona crossed her arms. "The Bureau thought *I* was this hero?" She seemed amused.

"I've already told them you are not," Khalil replied.

Her arms loosened and dropped. "I'm not?"

Khalil shook his head. "The Bureau has been looking for signs of a hero emerging across the known worlds. Hundreds of field agents have been sent out to investigate potentials. I was assigned to assess Xenia." He shrugged. "Xenia is no more. She was a Karassian construct, that is all. Now, the Bureau knows that, too."

"Wait," Sang said quickly. "The only way to fully assess a subject in the way you are describing is to meet them and talk to them."

"Yes."

"But..." Bellona said slowly, "...I was in the Ledan compound."

"Yes," Khalil repeated.

"You got yourself deliberately captured, just to *talk* to Bellona?" Sang asked.

"The Bureau have known and understood the true nature of Ledania and Appurtenance Services Inc. since before it was established. They had to know. They were paid to build the AIs that ran the memory programming. The Bureau is neutral, neither for nor against the Homogeny, as long as the money is good."

"Have you considered that *that* is why people think of the Bureau as monsters?" Bellona asked dryly.

"I *know* it is why," Khalil said flatly. "The Bureau arranged for the networks in the compound to show instabilities. I was already on Kachmar. They briefed me on the situation two hours before I was taken to the island to complete the contract."

"The Bureau knew the Karassians would wipe your memory," Sang said. "That is why you had the recall module implanted."

Bellona glanced at Sang, surprised.

"That was *their* precaution, not mine," Khalil said. "Of course the Karassians didn't kill me, because they cannot live without Bureau services and murdering Bureau agents is a quick way to lose all client privileges. However, the memory wipe was standard. Every other agent put in there for service work was treated the same way. The Bureau implanted the module in me so that my memories would be retained and I could therefore report back on my findings about Xenia." He blew out his breath. "Which I did, as soon as we arrived in orbit over Maggar, along with my resignation."

Bellona studied him. "Why is the Bureau looking for a hero? Do they think they will control the poor man?"

"The Bureau will be a part of the coming war," Khalil said quietly. "No one will get to sit it out, whether they want to or not. The Bureau wants to know who the hero is, so they can predict what happens next."

"You mean, so they can pick the right side?" Bellona shot back.

"Their explanation sounded far more altruistic," Khalil said. "Yet, I think that behind all the fancy explanations, the Bureau is scared. They're looking to survive, that is all."

"Their tactics do not paint them in flattering colors," Bellona said.

"Survival often is ugly."

"Why did you reach out to Bellona's family?" Sang asked. "When the module recovered your memories, that is the first thing you did."

Khalil's smile was rueful. "Even on the Bureau's home world, we heard about the disappearance of Bellona Cardenas. When I matched the DNA and realized who Xenia really was, I was shocked. Yet I was just an agent. The Bureau were going to reassign me. There was nothing I could do about it myself, so I sent the message. Then you showed up, Sang, when I had been braced for a fleet of Eriuman cruisers descending upon Kachmar."

"The Bureau will know you are here," Sang pointed out.

"You told them Xenia is not the one they seek, yet you followed her into the heart of Erium. They will not find that suspicious?"

"The Bureau know why I did it," Khalil said flatly. "Even they have not lost sight of the meaning of love."

Bellona looked away.

Khalil turned to face Bellona squarely. "That just leaves one question of my own, if you care to give me that much."

She lifted her chin and looked back at him steadily. "Ask."

"Who gave you the Bureau report?"

Bellona didn't answer.

Khalil nodded. "Then your father has succeeded in ejecting me from your life. I should congratulate him. Truth can be a slippery tool."

"I will not forget his role in this," Bellona said. Her voice was low. Controlled.

"I will have to be content with that." Khalil moved closer to her. He touched her cheek. Bellona was unmoved by his caress. "There has only ever been one direct lie between us," he said softly. "You asked who I answer to now I have left the Bureau. I told you no one. That was the lie." He bent and kissed her cheek. "I answered to you."

Bellona didn't move, even after he shut the door behind him, leaving Sang alone with her.

Chapter Eleven

Cardenas (Findlay IV), Findlay System, Eriuman Republic.

After Khalil's unremarked departure, the divide between Bellona and the rest of the family grew deeper. Bellona stopped talking to anyone, unless directly spoken to. She spent more time in her suite, reading histories and military treatises.

After five days of remaining locked in her suite, refusing all family communications and having food brought to her rooms, Sang suggested to Bellona that the inadequate combat skills they had developed would be refined by rigorous training. Bellona took a day longer to agree.

The first training session in the usual garden clearing — as all Bellona's training had been — left Sang trembling, their biological systems overtaxed and bruised. The next day, their muscles were uncooperative and aching despite painful massage to disperse the lactic acid.

That was also the day Bellona ordered Sang to her suite and gave them a list of research topics.

"Khalil Ready?" Sang said, repeating the last item.

Bellona's gaze was steady, despite the bloom of color in her cheeks. "Profile, history, psychoanalysis."

"You know why he did it," Sang pointed out. "Research won't provide a clearer answer. He had nothing to lose by giving you the truth."

"He wasn't who I thought he was. I want to find out just how wrong my assumptions were. I want to know if I can trust my own judgment. Just do it, Sang."

Sang complied.

While Sang completed the research projects, they moved through the house, taking care of Bellona's need for food, sleep and exercise, bringing back small pieces of news about the family while steadfastly refusing to provide the family with news about Bellona, as she had ordered. "Let them find out for themselves. If they're genuinely interested in my welfare, they will come, although I am not expecting anyone to appear at that door, Sang."

Sang was not surprised when her prediction proved accurate. They wondered if Reynard felt any regret when he realized how awry his stratagem had gone, that his efforts to remove Khalil had not sent Bellona into his arms for comfort, as any other daughter might have, from where he could nudge her in the direction of a more suitable partner.

Her psychological distance from the family, while still in close physical proximity, made Bellona's temper chancy. The combat training stepped up from three times a week to daily and Sang emerged from nearly every session with new aches, along with a respect for Bellona's strength and agility. Sang also appreciated that they were serving as an effective vent for Bellona's frustrations and submitted willingly to the pummeling.

When Sang suggested Bellona find accommodations somewhere in the city, away from the family homebase, she curtly refused. "I have things to do here, still."

Sang didn't repeat the suggestion. They were aware that in the night hours when the house was still and dark, Bellona would prowl through the rooms, looking for answers. The house AI and archivist reported to Sang each morning, believing it was helping Sang serve Bellona, per Max's orders, which was perfectly true.

Bellona spent hours in the kitchens. For most of those hours she lingered in the big store rooms, especially the cool rooms where preserves were made and kept. It was a policy in all the senior clans to keep their family homebases in a constant state of readiness for war and siege. Their cities could be destroyed. If rumors were true that the Karassians were building city-killers, that could wipe out a city-sized area in one blast from orbit, then those cities could be swept from the map in a few minutes. However, the homebases were always situated in the most defensible positions and could be rendered bomb-proof with a few short commands. Behind those indestructible walls, a family could live for years, if they made the correct preparations.

Sang had at first assumed that Bellona did not want to leave the comfort and hidden protection of the homebase. However, the Cardenas family store rooms were factory-sized buried rooms, where the produce from the gardens and farms and the largesse of subject families was kept and assiduously cycled. This was where Bellona crept for a short while each night.

Puzzled, Sang had ordered the house AI to take footage, which Sang had watched the next morning, their puzzlement evaporating.

Bellona was *sniffing* the supplies, looking for the spice, herb or compound that had tickled her lost memory. She wanted the pure source, to produce another recall. Because the olfactory sense was easily overwhelmed, she could only investigate a little at a time.

If she moved to another house in the city, she would not have access to the storerooms, unsupervised in the dead of night, as she did now.

Sang debated with themselves on whether the behavior was serving Bellona, or if they should intervene. No easy answer came to them, despite the same middle-of-the-night hours spent wrestling with the dilemma on journal pages.

Instead, Sang stepped up their own efforts to produce results for Bellona. They reported on progress each evening. They did not mention to Bellona that they were spending more time researching Khalil Ready's life, while ignoring most of the military profiles she had requested.

"He told me of his town being evacuated when he was a child," Bellona said. "There cannot be too many agrarian settlements concentrated within the equatorial zone, or that were grouped there before they could afford weather genera-tors. That was anywhere from twenty to forty years ago, Sang. There has to be a record of it. Even the free states keep records."

"For themselves, yes, but cooperative exchange of infor-mation is sluggish in the free states," Sang pointed out. "We cannot find a confirmed record for the birth of a child called Khalil Ready anywhere for the last sixty years. We could search further back…" Sang shrugged. Khalil Ready had youthful features and even the most gifted medical team could not make a seventy-year-old look young.

"Try any source, even the most illogical. And scour the records on Atticus again. An eleven-year-old boy cannot simply disappear, not even out there."

"A grown woman and highly visible member of the sen-ior clans of Erium disappeared from civilized space, ten years ago," Sang pointed out.

Bellona scowled. "I just want one confirming fact, Sang. You understand why, don't you?"

"You want to know he was not lying, the last day he was here."

"Thank you, Sang."

Sang left her to return to the task of unearthing the life of a minor in the free states, where "freedom" included the right to go unrecorded, undocumented and untrammeled by civic demands and responsibilities.

"They have other responsibilities, more intimate ones,"

Bellona pointed out when Sang brought the lack of documentation to her attention. "Survival is a sharper equation. When the local wildlife is eating one's summer harvest where it stands in the field, one doesn't stop to file an incident report. One gathers the neighbors and drives the wildlife into the next valley, or one doesn't eat that winter."

"Atticus is beyond such basics. It was settled nearly five hundred years ago."

"Even there, the right to live freely holds sway," Bellona said. "There are no social cushions, no government sponsored services. The people have the freedom to thrive or die trying, with no support."

Sang stared at her, startled. Sang was not the only one to dig into the history of the older planets in free space. "Khalil spoke of eating with the homeless. This would corroborate his testimony, would it not?"

Bellona winced.

"We apologize. We were still in witness mode when Khalil spoke of Atticus so his words are recorded as testimony. Although, we noted at the time that Atticus did not match with the story he told us about his childhood."

"Which is why I've decided he must have been evacuated at some stage, or moved for some reason. That reason is what you're looking for," Bellona finished.

Sang hesitated.

"What, Sang?"

"When Khalil spoke to me of his childhood, he said he

did not want the memories stimulated. He implied they were not all pleasant."

"All kids have unhappy memories. Just listening to their parents argue can sound like the end of the world if they're little enough." Bellona paused, considering. "You think it is more than that, though?"

Sang nodded. "The happy memory he shared…there was family there, somewhere. There had to be, for a child that age would not be so carefree without one. Yet on Atticus, he was alone."

Bellona considered it. "Maybe you should check the Karassian military annexation databases, Sang."

"That is not all. When we were on Kachmar, Khalil spoke of a brother."

"A *brother*?" Bellona sat up, startled, disturbing the tray of spiced tea. Lately, she had been requesting heavily spiced dishes for all her meals. She put her hand on the pot, steadying it. "Khalil never spoke of a brother. Not once."

"He only referred to him once, in passing. Benjamin, he called him. The most wanted man in Karassia."

Bellona looked pleased. "Did you run the enquiry?"

Sang nodded. "The only Benjamin in the free states the Homogeny has shown interest in is a Benjamin Arany, of no known allegiance to any free state. He is a maverick freeship captain who likes to harass both Karassian and Eriuman transports wherever he comes across them."

"So does every captain with a cargo to protect," Bellona

said, disappointment writing itself on her face. "They prefer to shoot first and get the hell out while the cruisers are trying to turn fast enough to get them in their sights."

"I believe that is where Max came up with his idea of small, agile fighters," Sang said. "He spent five years patrolling the borders of Eriuman. Arany, though, is not a typical freeship captain. He has a number of other freeships that look to him for leadership. As he spends his time harassing the Karassian military, they are most keen to...talk to him."

Bellona frowned. "Do you remember what Khalil said about heroes?"

"We do."

"What you just said about Arany makes me think of that. I wonder if the Bureau are looking for their hero out in free space?"

"I doubt that is ever something we would be able to find out. The Bureau are necessarily secret about how their algorithms and minds work."

"Apparently, not even the Bureau understands how they work," Bellona said. "Except for the interpreters." She shuddered. "Keep at it, Sang."

Sang searched, broaching unlikely record sources as Bellona had ordered. When Sang found the answer, they considered the implications for a whole day before presenting their findings to Bellona, who listened gravely.

"The military annexed a freeworld, twenty-six years ago," Sang told her. "It was agrarian, with no standing army, the arable land all concentrated around the equator and across only one of the six continents that transverse the equator."

"Why annex it?" Bellona asked, as Sang had anticipated.

"Hydrogen in pure diatomic state suspended in the southern ocean, in concentrations heavy enough to offset the cost of navigating the gravity well. Processors were built and a beanstalk pipeline to the outer atmosphere, all within ten years of conquering the planet."

"*Conquering*?" Bellona said sharply.

Sang nodded again. "The local farmers banded together and fought off the military landing craft. It was bloody, brutal and short. Afterward, every adult in the colony was rounded up and executed."

Bellona drew in a long slow breath. "The children...?"

"Put aboard a shuttle, that took them to the nearest free state and dumped them."

Bellona examined the front, then the back of her hand. "The year?"

Sang told her.

"That fits with Khalil's facts." Bellona shook her head. "Lately I have wondered why Erium continues this pointless war, then I hear about something like this and know why. Karassia is a disease, Sang. It will destroy us all if left to thrive."

"Yes, Bellona."

"And the name of the planet?"

"Before annexation, it was called Arcadia. Now, its official designation is Revati III."

"*Revati*?" Bellona stared at Sang, her eyes large. She grew pale. "Revati is an Eriuman possession." Her voice was stiff.

"Yes."

Her chest rose and fell quickly. "That is all," she said, her tone remote. Weak.

Sang left silently.

# #

For four consecutive days, Bellona cancelled combat training and did not emerge from her rooms, not even to wander the stores at night.

Sang waited and monitored the food that was sent to her suite. Too much of it came back untouched.

They considered the various ways Bellona might react to the facts of Khalil's childhood and the role of the Eriuman Navy in those events. She had received the confirmation she craved that Khalil had at least been truthful in the end. The truth, though, was not pleasant.

Sang hoped the experience would discourage Bellona from searching for a way to restore her lost memory of leaving Cardenas. The house AI report that she had stayed in her suite for four nights encouraged Sang.

When Bellona threatened her father with a ghostmaker she had smuggled past the house weapons filters, Sang learned they had been completely wrong.

About everything.

Chapter Twelve

Cardenas (Findlay IV), Findlay System, Eriuman Republic.

The house AI woke Sang with a screamed alert that made Sang tumble out of their cot while still half-asleep, trying to instantly assess the alarm and fumbling for clothes.

Dressed, Sang ran for the library, from where the house AI stated the weapons alert had originated. There were no other weapons in the house—at least, not traditional weapons. There were any number of innocent-looking objects and devices Sang could use as lethal weapons, thanks to Bellona's training. Until they had assessed the alarm for themselves, there was no need to signal their intent by picking up anything.

They were not the only ones woken. Family members were hurrying through the suddenly daylight-bright house, flinging on garments and suitable layers, shaking their heads, trying to orient themselves as they hurried to the library.

Sang met Iulia at the door and was startled to see her hair loose and brushing the back of her hips.

Then Sang looked into the library and shocked slithered through them.

Reynard Cardenas sat in the big green chair. He was fully dressed, in the clothes he had been wearing earlier in the evening, although his overshirt was rumpled. His face was devoid of any color. Sang wondered if more than shock was affecting him. He gripped the arms of the chair and did not move.

Bellona stood in front of him, a single-hand ghostmaker pointing at her father's chest. Her face was as pale as Reynard's.

"Tell them," she ordered him. Her voice was strained.

Reynard licked his lips. "There is no need for this. Put the gun down. We can speak freely without it."

Bellona laughed. The sound held no humor. "You *don't* talk. You avoid. You deny. You pretend everything is just fine. But you do not talk. This is the only way."

Iulia put her hand on Sang's back and shoved. Sang tripped forward and regained their balance, to find the muzzle of the ghostmaker pointed at them. They held their hands up as the household gathered at the door gasped.

"What do you wish your father to speak about?" Sang asked, keeping their voice calm and reasonable.

"He knows." Bellona swung the ghostmaker back to her father, who had been rising to his feet.

He sat down again. "She is hysterical," he said flatly. "Babbling about thugs and cologne and freeships. It's all nonsense."

"I'm not hysterical," Bellona said. "I'm calmer than I have

been for a long while, because now it is very clear."

"See?" Reynard said, spreading his hands. "She has ransacked my room, now she babbles inanities."

Sang glanced at the wall next to the big chair. A section of the paneling had been slid aside. There were such pockets of storage all over the room, most of them innocent. A stranger looking at this cupboard would consider the contents just as benign. Fluted decanters, squat bottles of spirit. Sitting in front of all of them was a smaller bottle that with a quick glance would be mistaken for more spirits, perhaps a rare hand blend.

The seal had been removed. Even from where they were standing on the far side of the room, Sang could detect the sharp, spicy scent.

Cologne.

The scent stirred in Sang the memory of the zesty dessert they had sampled while Bellona slumped at the table. The aromas were not identical, although they were closely related.

"This is the true source?" Sang asked, pointing.

Bellona worked her fingers on the grip of the ghostmaker. "I remember it all now." Her gaze was on Reynard.

Reynard did not ask what it was she remembered. He already knew. Sang could see it in his eyes.

"Sang," Bellona said quietly.

They looked at her expectantly.

"Count your toes. Count your nose. Breathe and repeat."

Sang staggered, as their balance shifted under the on-slaught of new memories spilling into their mind. No, not new. Hidden. Not repressed as human memories were, but inaccessible until this moment, when the key phrase un-locked them. They had been so carefully filed away that Sang had not been aware of their existence.

They realized that they were sitting in one of the hard vis-itor chairs, clutching the cushion to remain upright.

"What is wrong with it?" Iulia demanded from the en-trance to the room.

"That is shock, mother," Bellona said dryly. "Sang is re-membering now, too."

"Sort-review-analyze," Sang whispered. It was a mantra for times of confusion. Retreating to purely digital processing centered them. They looked for the beginning of the memory. The magic of time would give these strident memories coher-ence. They would make sense when arranged in order of oc-currence...

...the blow had not been entirely unexpected, yet the sound of hand slapping cheek was loud in the silent library. It seemed to echo in Sang's mind as all four of them froze in their positions by the shock of it.

Sang got their hand onto Max's shoulder as he tried to launch himself to his feet to defend his sister. Sang held him down.

Iulia, who knew her husband better than Max, remained still and silent, even as her throat worked and her hands crept beneath folds of her gown, to hide her reaction.

Bellona straightened, fingering the dark red mark on her cheek. Her eye on that side watered freely and her lips were swollen in the corner. She looked Reynard in the eyes, even though she trembled. The blow he had delivered had jarred her carefully piled hair from the top of her head and loose ringlets hung beside her face.

"Take it back," Reynard said, his voice strained. His arm was still raised. "Retract the statement."

Bellona gripped a fold of the yellow gown she was wearing. It was a pretty dress that Sang had always enjoyed seeing on her. Now she crushed the fragile fabric. "I won't marry Delben. I will join the Navy, like Max."

Reynard roared, a shapeless venting of rage. His hand lifted again and Bellona braced herself. She didn't step away or cringe.

"Father!" Max shouted, his voice breaking with a mix of emotions.

Reynard arrested the swing at the apex. He lowered his hand. "You can't join the Navy. You have no qualifications, no skills."

"I am combat trained." Bellona said it calmly.

Max sighed gustily. Now he understood why she had wheedled him into letting her train beside him.

Sang removed their hand and stepped back against the wall once more, where Riz and Wait stood.

"You are a woman. Your physical weakness is a handicap

the Eriuman Navy can live without," Reynard replied.

"On a cruiser, where the greatest physical demand is to push buttons?" Bellona asked, her voice rising.

"We're at war," Reynard shot back. "You have no idea what that means, what the true demands of such a career are. You've been protected all your life. *I* have made sure none of it touches you. You think this is an adventure, something novel to distract you for a while. Trust me, war is not what you think."

"Your father only has the best in mind for you," Iulia added softly.

"He wants me married to a Jaleesa so he can lock in the trade agreement. I'm not a fool, Mother!"

Iulia drew in a shaky breath and fell silent. Her eyes were huge as she looked at her husband for reassurance.

"The trade agreement is a pleasant side-effect, that is all," Reynard said heavily.

"Freedom is a pleasant side-effect of joining the Navy," Bellona replied.

Reynard's fury etched itself in his face once more. He curled his lowered hand into a fist. "You dare…!"

"That isn't fair, Bellona!" Iulia cried. "You have more rights and freedoms than any other citizen in history."

"The war you want to join ensures that," Reynard said. "The world beyond Erium is not the escape you seem to think it is. It is not a panacea."

"I'll never know that for myself, if you have your way,"

Bellona said. "Why won't you let me find out?"

Reynard, perhaps sensing the weight of the argument swinging his way, relaxed. His tone was gentler. Coaxing. "I have worked to provide a good life for you and Max. I ask only that you enjoy it. You are singularly unfit to survive beyond the borders of Cardenas, daughter. You have no experience of what it is like. The free states, the Homogeny…these places do not forgive mistakes. An error here among those who love you merely makes you look foolish. The same mistake, out there, will kill you."

Bellona looked away. She could not counter the argument because Reynard was right. She did not know what lay beyond Cardenas.

Sensing victory, Reynard smiled. "Now, take the day to think about Delben's proposal. It is a fair one. I have looked over the contract—"

"He gave it to *you*?" Bellona asked, her voice rising again.

Reynard frowned. "You would prefer a hired contractor vet the agreement?"

"I would prefer to have the choice!"

"Your ingratitude detracts from your character," Reynard snapped. "It comes perilously close to accusing me of illegalities."

"Your father is not forcing this on you," Iulia added. "Of course the choice is yours."

"Then I chose not to accept the agreement," Bellona said. She headed for the library door.

"I will let you think about it for a day or so," Reynard called after her. His tone implied he was granting her a favor.

Bellona didn't answer.

…the memory linked to the next. There were events in between, of course, although they were not lost memories. They were not linked together. Sang's mind turned to the next forgotten event.

Sort, review, analyze.

The summons to Max's rooms was a familiar one. Sang had been called for assistance in the middle of the night many times in the past. Max's infractions were mild, but Reynard had no patience for lack of discipline. Max had always called to Sang instead of his mother for help in covering up any indiscretions, even though Iulia was efficient at keeping vexing news from her husband. "She just gets that disappointed look on her face an' it makes me want to squirm," Max had told Sang the time he had needed to be poured into bed and nursed through his first hangover.

Sang moved through the house silently and slipped into Max's suite, wondering what fresh nonsense Max had dreamed up.

Bellona sat on the very edge of a chair, in the darkest corner. The dim light didn't fail to hide the blood covering her tunic, the cuts, scrapes and bruises forming on her arms, or the way the tunic was just barely covering her. The rents and tears would have revealed more, except that Max's big coat hung around her shoulders, hiding the worst of it.

Max was pacing. When Sang stepped in, he came over to them quickly. "I need you to reach out. A hidden channel, Sang."

"What happened?" Sang demanded.

"It doesn't matter," Max said quickly. "Can you do it?"

"A silent channel? Yes. Where to?"

"Cerce, to start."

"Ocantis IV?" Sang clarified. "That is a free state."

"Yes." Max crouched down in front of Bellona and lifted her hair to one side to check her face. "You'll need analgesic at the very least," he said gently. "Did they...do you need more specific medical intervention?"

"You mean, did they finish raping me?" Her voice was high and remote. Her gaze was glassy. "I killed him before he could."

Shock slithered through Sang. They stared. "You *killed* someone?"

Max got to his feet. "I should have thought of it sooner," he said, sounding vexed. "You'll find a body in the garden, where we train, Sang. You'll need to...deal with it. I don't know how such matters are handled, but I'm sure you do."

"There are ways," Sang said distantly. They moved closer to Bellona. "You really killed the man?"

Bellona blinked at him. "I had to."

"It's not important," Max said shortly. "Not now. Sang, the body. You can move around freely. I'll be noticed."

"Yes." Sang said. They made themselves turn and go.

The training area, when they reached it, was bare of anything but closely shaved grass, that shone silver in the light of the second moon, Cardenia. It was late and dew had formed. There were tracks through the dew, with a larger, darker patch of dry grass in one of the shadowed corners. Sang bent to examine it. The smell of blood, coppery and sharp, was distinct.

Sang spent the next fifteen minutes washing the blood away, then quartering the little area, looking for any other signs of disturbance and removing them. Then they returned to Max's suite.

Bellona was emerging from the ablutions area, her hair wet. The clothes she wore were Max's, although tucked into boots and cinched in with a belt, they were not ridiculously overlarge.

"We could collect more suitable clothes," Sang pointed out. "Or print fresh ones."

"No, nothing that leaves a trace," Max said quickly. "The garden, Sang?"

"There was a body, but it had been moved before we got there."

Max glanced at Bellona, his expression hardening.

"Did you think I made it up, little brother?" Bellona asked. She sounded calm, yet there was a wild look in her eyes, which were too large and too glassy.

"The confirmation is still a shock. *Murder*, Bell. The family can't protect you from that."

"Good," she said flatly.

Max threw out his hand. "You were only defending yourself!"

"If we could be made to understand what happened…?" Sang asked diffidently.

"I went to the garden to meet Max for late night training," Bellona said. "We set it up days ago."

"You cancelled on me," Max said.

Bellona shook her head.

"What was the form of the cancellation?" Sang asked.

"The House AI told me Bellona was staying in her room for the night."

"Such a channel can be broached easily," Sang pointed out. "The true origin of the message masked. We will examine it, later."

"It set Bellona up," Max said angrily. "Whoever they were, they targeted her. Four of them."

"I think it was four. It was dark," Bellona said quietly. "They came out of the shadows and they used my name. They knew who I was." She paused, then said reflectively, "It didn't seem to scare them, knowing who I was."

"They attacked you?" Sang said, sparing her the description.

She nodded. "Then, when the shock passed, when I realized it really was happening…well…I just…reacted."

"And killed a man," Max whispered.

"Then I came here," Bellona said, looking around the

suite.

"You were right to come to me," Max said. He stopped in front of her again. "You're going to have to leave. You know that, don't you?"

Bellona swallowed. "That's why you asked Sang about a channel to the free states."

"I'll take you to New Edsel, first," Max said. "Everyone is used to me heading off there."

"They believe you have an unofficial lover there," Sang offered.

Max rolled his eyes. "This family and its conspiracies..." he muttered. "It will do for now. I have a skiff there, Bellona. I know a freeship captain who operates from Cerce who owes me a favor and I can get you onto her ship once it is in local space. Captain Wang will take you back to the free states."

"Then what?" It was a whisper.

Max closed his eyes briefly. "I don't know, Bell. I don't *want* to know. You're going to have to make your own way after that."

Bellona's chin quivered. She pressed her lips together to make it stop. Then she nodded. "Very well." Her shoulders under the big jacket straightened. "We'd better hurry," she added.

They had stolen into the night, after Max had left a message with the house AI to let everyone know he would be in New Edsel for a week. They took nothing with them that

166

would provide clues later.

It took six hours by ground car to reach New Edsel. Max would not risk a semi-ballistic, for they were noisy on take-off and tended to draw attention. People stopped to watch them crawl up into the higher atmosphere, growing smaller and smaller.

The ground car wound through the hills, while Max slept and Bellona watched the night fade through the observation ports. Sang remained plugged into the communications satellites and switched their way through shortbands, changing swiftly, adding random cut-offs, always aiming for Cerce and the established communications net surrounding the Ocantis system. The Cerce AI was friendly and trusting, accepting that Sang was Max without a quiver.

Captain Tatiana Wang of the *Hathaway* was known to the Cerce AI. It accepted the sealed communications bullet and assured Sang it would pass it on as soon as the *Hathaway* was within reach. Then it asked for a return channel.

Sang hesitated, weighing the options. Then Sang curtly told it there would be no return possible. Sang disconnected, leaving the AI troubled. Sang was confident the message would be delivered as promised, though, for that was the AI's function and to not fulfil its function would invoke stressors. AIs did not like uncertainty.

New Edsel was a sleepy little town in the prairies, with charming historical buildings and Cardenas family offshoots that traced their ancestors back to the original Cardenas settlers. The high flat plains offered excellent landing fields and the original landing site was thought to be somewhere nearby, although no traces of the historic location had been found and records were hazy.

The flat land attracted a thriving air industry and many lucrative support businesses catering to pleasure craft and their occupants. Max had been smart to keep his skiff here. He would be one more Cardenas among a great many others and could come and go with relative privacy.

As the ground car wound through the downtown area, Max sat up and rubbed sleep from his eyes and asked Sang to reach out to the skiff and get it ready.

Bellona showed no sign of interest in the preparations. Her gaze remained on the view beyond the port. Even when the car pulled up next to the little runabout, she didn't stir.

Sang was familiar with the skiff, for they had been instrumental in Max's getaways in the past. "The skiff is not equipped for no-atmosphere maneuvering," Sang pointed out.

"It is air-tight and it has an emergency thruster. I just need to get up high enough to meet the *Hathaway*, then use the thruster to get back down low enough to drop."

"And how will you dock?" The skiff had nothing resembling an airlock.

"That's why I'm using the skiff," Max said. He helped Bellona out of the car. "It will fit inside the *Hathaway*'s cargo hold."

"And if the hold already contains cargo?"

Max looked at Sang. He was still young, still fresh with youth and energy, but the look in his eyes was one Sang had not seen before. It was an older man looking at Sang. A wiser one. "I'll make it worth Wang's time to drop the load."

Sang nodded. "We will wait here with the car, for your return."

Max nodded and eased Bellona into the skiff, then inserted himself, too. Sang watched the little vehicle take off, then ascend almost vertically, leaving a clear trail in the early morning sky.

That was the last time Sang saw Bellona. Ten years would pass before they saw her again.

#

Sang pressed their fingers to their temple. Their head hurt.

"Sang," Bellona called. "Sit up. I need your help with this."

Sang nodded and tried to obey. They moved slowly. "Max...locked the memories away. After. When we got back from New Edsel."

Bellona glanced at her father and adjusted her aim, then looked back at Sang. "Max told me what he was going to do. He gave me the phrase. I only remembered it now. Tonight." She turned to face Reynard once more. "Max knew all along. He lied to protect me. I hope you appreciate that."

Reynard swallowed. The skin around his throat moved

loosely. It was the flabby flesh of an old man. Sang had never thought of Reynard as old before.

"I don't know what you're talking about," Reynard said.

"You *do* know. You know exactly what this is about. You've been waiting for this moment to arrive for ten years," Bellona told him. "You worked to cover it up. You lied, too. More than Max did and for far worse reasons. Max was at least protecting someone else."

"Bellona, for the stars' sake..." Iulia protested. "Please put that...*thing* down and let us talk civilly."

"Reynard has given up any rights to a civil conversation," Bellona said. "Ask him, mother."

"I will not play this game," Iulia said firmly. "I am going to bed."

Sang glanced at her. Iulia had not moved from the spot. None of the others ranged behind her looked as if they wanted to leave, either.

Sang turned their gaze back to Reynard. They were not certain why they must watch the man, except that Bellona's need to hold him at gunpoint seemed warning enough.

Reynard looked less threatening than he had ever had in the past. He looked tired. Resigned. Except that Sang had never seen Reynard Cardenas give up. His relentlessness and drive had made him the prime member of the most senior family in the clan. His absolute confidence in his decisions cemented him there.

So Sang remained wary.

Reynard's gaze slid back to Bellona. Measured her.

Bellona swapped hands on the gun. "Sang doesn't know all of it. Max didn't know all of it. Even *I* didn't know all of what happened that night, until I smelled the cologne you'd so carefully hidden away. Then it all came back. You were there that night. You watched it all happen."

Sang's lips parted as shocked made their jaw sag.

"Watched *what*?" someone whispered, behind them.

Reynard's gaze didn't shift from Bellona. "I still don't know what you're talking about. You're not making sense."

"For the first time in a long time, I'm making perfect sense," Bellona assured him. "The Bazaar from Erium was here that week. The whole city was going crazy. You were just as bad, buying clothes and trinkets and baubles. You bought colognes, too. That was why I didn't recognize the scent as yours that night. I smelled it, though. It passed through the trees you were hiding behind. I even paused, when the scent reached me. It was so very distinct. Tell me, *Father*, when you hired the men from the Bazaar to rape me, did you intend merely to see they earned their money, or are you a voyeur too?"

Iulia moaned sickly.

Reynard swallowed.

Bellona nodded, as if that was confirmation enough. "We are at another impasse, aren't we? You saw me murder a man. It must have been a shock to you, to see me fend for myself. You've always had such a low opinion of my ability to do that. That's why I know you arranged for those men to intimidate me into staying safely inside the family nest, where I could be protected and guarded and shoved into Delben's arms. I think the clan would find your behavior objectionable in their leader."

For the first time, Reynard reacted. He flinched.

Bellona smiled. "You will make sure that none of this ever leaves this room. You know what the consequences will be if you do not." She lowered the ghostmaker. "Sang."

Sang got to their feet. Slowly.

"Where do you think you're going?" Reynard demanded.

"I'm leaving." Bellona looked over her shoulder. "Don't try to stop me. Don't tell Wait to try, either. You'll both regret it."

Reynard swallowed again.

Bellona beckoned to Sang. They turned and followed her from the room.

It was an echo of another long night. The ground car wound its way through the hills toward New Edsel. Bellona looked through the port windows, while Sang arranged a communications channel. This time, the channel was far easier to set up, because it was Eriuman at both ends. That didn't shorten the distance, though. It took three hours for the channel to cohere.

Sang shook Bellona gently, as they cast the channel and

built a screen at the front of the car, where Bellona could see it.

Max tilted his head, his dark eyes taking in the interior of the ground car and Bellona's appearance. "What happened?"

"I remembered, Max." Her voice was raw.

Max sat back. He didn't ask what she had remembered.

"Why didn't you tell me?" Bellona demanded.

Max let out a heavy breath. "I was so pleased when you couldn't remember what happened," he confessed. "I thought the whole thing could be forgotten."

"It didn't occur to you that I would keep digging until I found it?"

Max screwed up his nose. "You were always stubborn, but you had a short attention span, too. Five minutes, five days, with some new trinket or lover or toy and you'd be done, bored and onto the next thing. No, I didn't think you would ever keep at it like this."

Bellona sighed. "There are so many gaping holes in my life now, Max. So many things out there I don't remember that might yet come back to haunt me. You should have told me about this."

Max shook his head. "Why would I do that? You look ill, Bell. You look as though you've been kicked in the guts. Is knowing the truth worth it? It hasn't gained you a thing."

"I look like I've been kicked in the guts because I have," she said shortly. "There's a thing you don't know about that night. Father arranged it, to demonstrate how weak and useless I really was. An object lesson to keep me in line."

Max ran his hand over his shorn head. "That's…" He cleared his throat. "You're *sure*?" he breathed.

"I think I always knew, deep down." Bellona gave a small laugh. "Do you know he was so certain of his power and my uselessness that he never destroyed the cologne? He hid it, instead, which means he knew I would identify him by it. Yet he didn't get rid of it. He was that complacent and that tight fisted. The stars would misalign if he actually threw something useful away."

Max shook his head. "I have no idea what you mean about cologne and I don't have time to talk about it. Bellona, this is…I have to think about it."

"I need to know I can trust you, Max. I thought I did. I want to, but this…"

"You know why I lied."

"You need to stop protecting me. It's just tripping me up."

Max laughed. "Tripping you up on your way to where?"

"I don't know. I've left the city. I'll let you know when I find somewhere to stop. I have some thinking to do."

"So do I," Max admitted. His face was troubled. "This changes things."

"Yes," she said simply.

Max looked over his shoulder at something not visible within the screen. "Time to go pretend I run this ship, Bell. Sang, stay with her."

"Yes, Max."

The screen popped and disintegrated.

#

They spent four days in New Edsel, while Bellona took a measure of the town and began speaking to marketers about properties in the area.

That was where the news reached them that the body of Maximilian Cardenas Scordino de Deluca, Captain of the *Decimus*, had been found on Antini.

Chapter Thirteen

Cardenas (Findlay IV), Findlay System, Eriuman Republic.

It took nearly three weeks for an investigation to be completed by the Eriuman Navy. In that time, Naval officers from the criminal justice division haunted Cardenas, combing through family records and interviewing everyone.

A cadre of them arrived in New Edsel two days after they had received the news. They were polite but insisted that Bellona speak with them. Bellona, in turn, insisted that Sang be included in the interview.

The Lieutenant, Hult, glanced at Sang. It was the first time she had looked directly at Sang since stepping into the foyer of the boarding house where Bellona was currently living. The lieutenant brushed down her uniform with a sweep of her hand. "Very well," she said carelessly.

The interview took place aboard the Navy shuttle that had grounded in the middle of New Edsel's town square, cracking and scorching the fused cobblestones and forcing townspeople to use the side roads to reach their destinations. Commerce had virtually halted. Sang suspected the townspeople would blame Bellona for that. They tucked the thought away for later consideration as Bellona was shown a seat located directly in front of the lieutenant's.

Lieutenant Hult laid one hand over the other, both of them on her crossed knee. The posture displayed the shining toe of her boot. "May I first offer my condolences on the loss of your brother, Miss Cardenas?"

"Thank you," Bellona said stiffly. It was the same tone she had used with every single person who had dared to mention Max in the last two days. As most of the townspeople were related by some degree, most of them had stopped to speak to Bellona.

"We will miss Maximilian," Hult added. "He provided an insight and flair to naval affairs that was a breath of fresh air in some corners." Hult's smile was small, but it was there.

Bellona's eyes narrowed. "You knew Max?"

Hult gave a very small shrug of her shoulders. "A little."

Sang registered the lie.

"Does that make you an unsuitable investigator?" Bellona asked.

"It makes me keener to get to the bottom of this... mystery." Hult crossed her arms. "What can you tell me about Max's last hours on Cardenas?"

"What can you tell me about how he died?"

"That is not a part—"

"It is now," Bellona said. She waited.

Hult smiled. "Miss Cardenas, I have been an investigator in this division for a very long time. There are certain kinds

177

of information that cannot be shared with members of the public, not even close relatives or siblings, if the sharing of that information might jeopardize ongoing military matters. That is the reason the Navy investigates, not a civilian authority."

"The civilian authority being the family enforcers," Bellona replied. "Tell me, have you interviewed my father, yet?"

"As a matter of courtesy, we spoke with your father as soon as we landed." Hult seemed to be amused by Bellona's attempts to steer the conversation.

"Did you tell my father how Max died?"

"*Some* facts were shared."

"Share those facts with me, then."

"Your father can tell you what he knows."

"I asked you."

"Miss Cardenas—"

"Call me Bellona." Bellona crossed her legs to match Hult. "It does not seem to have occurred to you, Lieutenant Hult, that with Max's death, I am the sole remaining heir of my father's estate."

Hult's smile was very small. "I hear that you and your father are recently estranged. Perhaps that inheritance is not as certain as you imply."

Bellona nodded. "You're good at your job. That pleases me. It means you will get to the bottom of this. Max called me stubborn, lieutenant. My father has recently learned exactly what that means. If you wish your investigation to proceed smoothly, I suggest you not attempt to discover the extent of my stubbornness today. If you have already learned about my exit from the family, then you will also know where I have been for the last ten years and what I have been doing."

"I heard, yes," Hult said evenly.

Sang stared at Bellona, surprised. It was not usual for her to raise the subject of Xenia herself. Now she was using it like a prod.

"Tell me how Max died," Bellona said. "Then I will tell you what I know."

Hult considered her. "Be careful what you ask for, Bellona."

"I have learned that truth is less dangerous than ignorance, no matter how unpleasant it may be. Tell me. Did he die inside the Pleasure Dome?"

Hult hesitated. Then, "No. Just outside it, although his register shows he was inside at one point."

"How did he die?"

Hult shook her head. "Really—"

"Tell me," Bellona demanded.

Hult drew in a breath and let it out. "His limbs were severed. He was gutted. Then he was left to bleed out, while his remains were piled in front of him." Hult looked away, then brought her gaze firmly back to Bellona. "You insisted," she added.

Bellona sat very still for a moment. "Then it was not my

father who arranged this."

Hult looked stunned. "You thought your *father* did this?"

Bellona nodded. "It was a possibility," she said coolly. "Max knew something that made him dangerous to my father. You look shocked, Lieutenant. Did you think the head of the Scordini clan would be a benevolent man?"

Hult gnawed at her lip, her doubt plain. "I did not assume that, although I have never heard it spoken about so openly, especially by an inner family member." Her eyes narrowed. "Did this dangerous knowledge have something to do with why you left the city?"

"Yes," Bellona said flatly. "The manner of Max's death, though…that is not the way my father would have arranged it. He loved Max. He would not have wanted him to suffer. It would have been quick and clean. Plus, he has made no move against me and I have the same knowledge."

Hult looked uncomfortable and a little ill. Perspiration appeared on her upper lip and she wiped it away. "There is nothing to indicate that Reynard Cardenas was involved. Antini is a long way from here."

"It is in free space, possibly the one truly neutral city in the entire galaxy," Bellona said. "I am aware of the reason why."

"The Pleasure Dome," Hult said. Her mouth curled up. "Free sex with whatever partner you want, whenever you want it, however you want it. Karassians and free staters and Eriumans, biobots, androids. Every depravity is catered to, without question."

"Is it possible…?" Bellona began. She looked at Hult. "Even the Karassians with their genetic enhancements have never been able to stamp out the worst of human nature. Is it possible a customer was interested in necrophilia and the Dome took Max to meet the customer's demands?"

Hult paled. "I have an investigator with a stronger stomach than mine looking into that right now."

"Good." Bellona nodded again. "What was Max doing that far inside free space?"

Hult cleared her throat. "His aide says he took an abrupt leave of absence and jumped on a bus doing a Kalay-Antini-Cerce-Xindar run."

"Max on a public bus?" Bellona shook her head. "Does that not strike you as unlikely? You knew him."

Hult smiled. "It did seem odd to me," she admitted. "However, Max was, above all, practical. A public bus is just that—*public*. If he thought he was in danger, then taking a free state shuttle would ensure no move was made against him while he was in transit." Hult scowled. "I don't suppose you know which of those stops would have been his destination? He bought a round ticket."

"Cerce," Bellona replied. "He knew someone there."

"Captain Tatiana Wang?"

Bellona raised a brow. "Yes."

Hult studied her. "Then you don't know."

Bellona shook her head. "I know she's dead."

"The *Hathaway* was lost, a week after you disappeared from Cardenas," Hult added.

Bellona dropped her gaze to her knee. "The Karassians destroyed her, straight after taking me." Her jaw flexed. "That is why no one came looking for me."

"There was nothing left to trace you by," Hult said. "Although Max made me keep looking for years afterward. Any clue, any hint."

Bellona considered her. "Then why would he be heading for Cerce, so soon after learning…about Reynard?"

"That is a question I would like answered, too," Hult said. She hesitated. "Normally, I would not share this with a civilian, but you're not really a civilian anymore, are you?"

Bellona grimaced. "What do you want to share?"

"A concern. Even if it was not your father who did this, it is possible that the reason you left the family is the same reason that got Max killed, in some indirect way I have yet to uncover. You could be in danger yourself."

"The thought had crossed my mind," Bellona admitted. "Although I pity the fool who tries to attack me."

Hult's laugh pushed out of her in a breathy gasp, as if it caught her by surprise. Her gaze met Bellona's. Then she got to her feet. Bellona followed suit. Hult thrust out her hand and Bellona gripped Hult's elbow.

Sang moved to open the door. Hult shot them a startled glance, as if she had forgotten Sang was there. She pulled herself together and let go of Bellona's arm. "I will be completing the investigation as swiftly as possible, although I should warn you that I do not foresee a conclusive outcome. There are too many questions and too few answers." Hult grimaced. "That is not something I shared with your father."

"A smart decision," Bellona told her. "Thank you for your time, Lieutenant."

Hult nodded.

Sang held the door for Bellona, while noting the inconsistency. It had been Hult who had demanded Bellona's time. Apparently, Hult had forgotten that.

# #

New Edsel stopped speaking to Bellona after that. They could not refuse a Cardenas service and had no troubles taking her money. They simply stopped talking to her. Sang overheard snatches of conversation as Bellona passed by and put it together.

"They believe you are involved in Max's murder. They can see no other reason why the investigators sought you out so quickly, or why you have left the family home. They think Reynard cast you out."

"I *am* involved in Max's murder," Bellona said. "I just don't know how or why yet, but I know in my gut that this is my fault."

"You have no evidence of that," Sang said sharply. "Neither does New Edsel. Maybe Max simply wanted to visit the Dome and fell in with the wrong partner."

Bellona rolled her eyes. "Sang, really, in all the time you have known Max, all the scrapes you got him out of, did you ever catch a hint of such perverse tastes?"

Sang grimace and shook their head. "Partners aplenty, including, we suspect, Lieutenant Hult. Just nothing like that."

"Exactly," Bellona replied. "We will just have to put up with New Edsel ignoring us. I refuse to go back to the city until I absolutely have to and there's no point in finding somewhere else until after."

Sang didn't ask what "after" meant. The coming rites hung over them both just as the late summer monsoon clouds gathered overhead, turning every day into a dim sauna. They waited out the days until word came. The investigation had been closed, Max's remains returned to Cardenas and the public interment would be held in three days' time.

#

The city was filled to overflowing. Every inn, every boarding house, every hotel, was at capacity. On the five hour journey to the city, Sang connected with every reputable and less reputable accommodation in the city with no success. Bellona was philosophical. "We have the ground car. We can take turns sleeping in it, if we have to, but I don't expect to be in the city long enough to make sleep a priority."

The rites were held in the same grand hall as Bellona's homecoming. There, all similarities ended. There were far more people thronging the street, surging in waves toward the hall, trying to get as close as possible. There were vastly more people inside the hall, too. There was no shouting. No cheering. The street was eerily quiet for having so many people squashed into it. The ground car pilot could not find a way through the morass, so Sang moved behind the controls and took command. They were more ruthless about nosing up against thighs and hips and clearing a path that way. It would be better to save Bellona as much walking as possible.

It became impossible to move forward any farther. They got out of the car and pushed their way through the crowd then, finally, up the wide steps to the hall itself. There were human sentries and greeters before the doors. Everyone moving into the hall was being scanned.

Gaubert was standing with the guards, his expression somber. When he saw Bellona, his jaw tightened. He pulled her aside. Sang moved closer.

"You are not expecting to join the family on the dais, are you?" he whispered loudly.

Bellona shook off his hand from her arm. "I am here for my brother, Gaubert. That is all. I can say my farewells from the back balcony as well as I can from the dais."

Gaubert shook his head. "Your registration has been removed from the inner security zones. Neither you nor Sang will be allowed upstairs. You can join the general population in the hall, although…" He looked over his shoulder, into the hall itself. "I would hurry, if I were you. There isn't a lot of room left in there."

Bellona opened her mouth to argue. Sang could see the anger glinting in her eyes.

Gaubert looked at her steadily, waiting for her outburst.

Sang calculated the pressure of the bodies ahead, put their arm around Bellona's waist and forced her forward, up the final broad step and into the crowd, shepherding her along as one would help the feeble or disabled.

Bellona gasped at the sudden movement, just barely keeping her feet under her. She glared at Sang.

They shook their head. "Anywhere inside will do. Max will understand. He might even approve."

Bellona remained silent and pushed ahead as Sang was doing. It was a struggle to get through the great doors. Finally, they passed under the lintel and into the cavernous hall beyond. The pressure of bodies slackened and they worked their way to one side of the room, away from the surge of people pushing through the doors.

Bellona finally looked up at the dais and sucked in a deep breath, making everyone nearby glance at her. Some took a second glance, startled. She had been recognized.

The flame that was the symbol of Max's life was already burning atop the pedestal. Surrounding the flame were all the familiar faces. Sang could name them all without hesitation—Reynard's brothers and sisters, their spouses and their off-spring. It was a crowded dais.

Directly behind the pedestal stood Reynard Cardenas. He

looked as though he had aged a decade since they had been gone from the city. His hair, which had still held black locks, was now almost pure silver. He was staring at the flame, with the gaze of a man searching for answers.

Iulia stood next to Reynard, her head covered by a heavy veil. There was at least a body's width between them.

The twelve chimes began and the hall fell into complete silence.

Bellona hung her head.

Sang rested their hand on her shoulder and leaned close to murmur in her ear. "Guilt will not serve you here. Watch the flame go out. Honor him. Let everyone around you see that honor."

Bellona raised her chin again and glanced at Sang. Then she looked ahead, her gaze steady. She did not move throughout the ceremony. When the flame was extinguished, she flinched, but that was the only reaction she gave.

#

On the way back to New Edsel, the rains began. Water thundered on the roof of the ground car and turned the last of the day into instant night and the silent interior into a muffled enclosure. Bellona appeared unmoved by the torrent. She had not spoken since the end of the ceremony. Neither did she sleep.

Sang did not disturb her reflections. They attempted to pick up the strings of various research projects. Instead they found their thoughts circling around Max. They were intrusive thoughts. Petty ones. Max's first hangover and the combined efforts of the family to hide the event from Reynard. Max's first steps as a child, tottering to reach not his mother, but Bellona, still only a child herself yet already his constant companion. There were many memories that occurred to Sang. If they wanted to, they could review Max's life moment by moment, a luxury that humans did not get to enjoy.

Sang recognized the desire to sink into review for what it was. Avoiding decisions would not help Bellona now. Descending to helplessness because the source of direction had gone would be a waste, which the Scordinii deplored.

We use the parameters that best suit the assignment. How many times had Sang said that to others? The assignment had not changed. Max had been clear. *Help Bellona.* Only the parameters had changed. Sang would not receive more explicit instructions. They must devise those for themselves.

Sang stared ahead, while in their mind they built a matrix of possible parameters, nodes of decision, potential outcomes and consequences.

When the car pulled up next to the boarding house in New Edsel, the matrix was as complete as current information could make it.

It was very dark outside. It was late and most of the lights, both external and internal, had been doused for the night. What few lights remained reflected off the wet surfaces, making them gleam. Nothing moved in the narrow street.

Bellona stirred and unsealed the car. Instantly, the sound of rain leapt and she recoiled, as if she had noticed the rain only now.

Sang went ahead, to unlock the outer door of the boarding house so she did not have to linger on the sidewalk. The rain was heavy enough that Sang was instantly soaked, even moving the few meters to the door. They palmed the lock and pushed. The door didn't open.

Vexed, Sang tried again. A lot of water on the palm could interfere with the pad's function.

Bellona stepped up beside them. "What's the matter?" She had to raise her voice to be heard.

"It won't open." Sang stepped back out onto the sidewalk to look up at the second floor, where the boarding house owner had their apartment. There were no lights showing on that floor. Even the minimal security lights that were usually left on in the front foyer were extinguished, for nothing showed through the ground floor windows.

Bellona pressed her hand against the pad and pushed. The door remained closed. She tried again, then grabbed the handlebar and put her shoulder to the door.

Sang watched as she threw herself against the door over and over. Under the noise of the rain, they could hear her swearing. Each bump against the door grew harder and heavier, until she was ramming herself against it, making the bomb-proof door rattle in its sealed frame. The impact drove her backward.

She grew still, staring at the door. The rain was pouring off her in rivulets. Then she ran at the door and kicked it. The kick used up the last of her energy. She put her head against the door and closed her eyes.

Sang hesitated. They knew what had to be done, only there was no one here to take the step. There was only Sang.

They moved to the door and eased Bellona away from it. They put their arms around her and spoke just loudly enough for her to hear above the rain. "It only feels like you are alone."

Bellona hid her face against their shoulder. Her arms tightened around their neck.

#

The next day, Sang sold the ground car to a grasping trades-man who understood exactly what he was buying while pretending ignorance to drive the price down. Sang let him push the price down to just above Sang's bottom line, then walked.

The trader caught up with Sang at the entrance to the trading post across the road and coaxed Sang back. Sang let him add another fifteen percent to the price then they grasped each other's arms.

They used the money to buy essentials, as all their current possessions, clothes and supplies were still in the boarding house that had expelled them. Neither of them was interested in trying to get anything back.

They met Bellona at the eatery in the main square and

listed their purchases, while Bellona played with the hot cakes on her plate.

"Semi-ballistic?" she asked, when Sang itemized the tickets. "To where?"

"Abilio."

"Where is that?"

"Tertius." The third continent was in the southern hemisphere. "It will be winter there."

"Why Abilio?"

Sang grimaced. "It was the closest to a random flag on the map that I could generate. There is absolutely nothing connecting you to Tertius or Abilio. I have no idea what is there. It has no real history and barely enough infrastructure to support fewer than a handful of permanent buildings. We'll have to figure it out when we get there. Money is going to be the first priority."

Bellona looked at them. "You're using first person singular."

Sang nodded. "Where you and I are headed, they won't be used to androids. They certainly won't understand the neutral gender."

Bellona looked at them for another long moment. "Don't pretend, Sang. I'm sick of illusions. Let them deal with the truth. It's not up to you to ease their way."

Sang drew in a breath, for calmness and to center themselves. "I'm not pretending."

Chapter Fourteen

Angylia free state, Angyl moon, Yu System.

Ferid kept the man awake with stimulants injected directly into his hypothalamus, taking care not to disturb the buildup of plaque and detritus so the effects of sleep deprivation would be acute. It blunted the man's executive decision-making processes, keeping him pliant.

The man's medical knowledge meant he knew what Ferid was doing, which added a degree of fun to the whole tiresome exercise. Ferid couldn't remember his name. He had identified him by the metal finger, an oddly biobotic feature to find in a free-stater. Three weeks of drinking in the right bars on the right planets had led Ferid to the tidbit: One of Arany's crew had a metal finger. After that, it had taken less than a day to find the man...and he had a wife.

Ferid displayed the woman for the man to see. It had been difficult deciding how much pain he should put the woman through before offering the man the deal. Too much, and he might decide Ferid was lying about letting the wife go if he talked. Too little, and he might decide that Ferid didn't really mean to kill her.

The dilemma was another novel aspect to the project. It had provided uncertainty. Finally, though, Ferid had found the balance that provided optimum persuasion.

The man blubbered, torn by competing loyalties.

Then Ferid thought of what to say. Awed at his own brilliance, Ferid leaned closer to the smelly man. His smile was genuine. "No one has to know it was you. Arany will never learn about this." He had to raise his voice to be heard over the breathless moaning of the woman, which destroyed the intimacy of the moment.

The man's bloodshot eyes gazed at him. Ferid watched hope dawn.

"You'll let her go?"

"Yes." She would not be alive when he did let her go, but he would most certainly release her.

The man looked away, toward his wife. He wept again. "What do you want to know?"

#

The Bonaventura, Free space, Xindar-Coria Confluence.

"Um…boss?" Natasa's voice carried across the bridge.

Benjamin Arany looked up from the chart he was studying and raised a brow.

Natasa straightened up from where she had been bent over the shoulder of the intern on the scanners. "They're here."

"Erium?"

She nodded. Her elongated eyes narrowed even farther. "You *sure* you want to do this?"

"I don't think I've been completely sure since I kissed Maureen Owenzky behind the woodpile when I was twelve." Arany dismissed the chart and got to his feet. "We'd better come about and hold."

Natasa rolled her eyes. "Maybe we should just duck and run as usual. I mean…" She glanced around the bridge and moved closer, so she could lower her voice. "Word is, the Eriumans are more pissy than usual. Some royal son of theirs got killed and they're grumpy about it."

Arany nodded. "Maximilian Cardenas. He died in free space, Natasa. That's why they're grumpy. They think we did it. You might want to at least try to keep up with the news."

Natasa grinned. "We didn't?"

"Kill him? I don't think anyone in free space is that stupid."

"Maybe they didn't know who they had under the knife."

"The purple uniform should have told them. You don't fuck with the Eriumans."

"Right. So why are we fucking with them, boss?" She pointed at the scanner screens the intern had up. The blip was big.

"Cruiser?"

"The *Jovian*."

Arany was pleased. The *Jovian* was one of the big ones,

retrofitted to carry fighters in the hold. "Are they shouting at us yet?"

"Boss, you're on their wanted list. They're not going to shout. They're going to shoot."

Arany looked over his shoulder. "Ready, Dex?"

Dex had his hands over his dashboard, hovering. He nodded.

Arany leaned on the navigation table. "Let's do this."

#

Eriuman Naval Vessel Jovian, Free space, Xindar-Coria Confluence.

Captain Sher Carosa tilted his head, baffled. "Is he...just sitting there?" he asked of everyone, as he studied the screen showing the small, shiny dot.

Pramoda lifted his head. "They scanned us. They know we're here."

Carosa frowned. "It *is* the *Bonaventura*, yes?"

"Confirmed."

Carosa sighed. "Free-staters..." He signaled to the midshipman, who turned to murmur to the coordinators under his command. "Arany is too critical to ignore," Carosa told Pramoda.

Pramoda watched the mid-shipman. "Fighters launched," he confirmed.

Carosa watched on the screen as the swarm of little fight craft speared across open space, heading for the *Bonaventura*.

"More ships have appeared, sir," Pramoda said calmly.

"More?" Carosa was startled. "How many?" Now he could see them on the screen. More pinpoints of light, gathering around the *Bonaventura*. "Magnify!"

The screen zoomed. Now the ships were clear—a motley cloud of freighters and converted ex-military vehicles, reclaimed public transports…in short, the junk of the galaxy.

"Forty-six ships, sir," Pramoda said. "Forty-seven," he added as another one appeared.

"Forty-seven freeships, all in one place," Carosa breathed.

"And they're not shooting at each other, either," Pramoda pointed out.

"They're turning!" one of the bench coordinators called out.

On the screen, the forty-seven free ships were all orienting themselves. One only oriented a ship when they intended to traverse space. Null-space jumps could be taken from anywhere.

"Are they attacking?" Pramoda asked, sounding amused.

Carosa sat up, his heart giving a little squeeze. "When will the fighters reach them?"

"They're closing," the mid-shipman said.

Carosa rolled his eyes. "How *soon*?"

The mid-shipman looked down at his team. "Twenty seconds."

It was a tense twenty seconds. Carosa stared at the screen, his mind racing, trying to figure out Arany's ultimate intention. They could engage with the fighters, but what would it prove? They could not take on a cruiser, not even forty-seven of them.

The freeships leapt forward, all of them keeping together in a tight formation that Carosa had time to admire for the coordination needed for such a maneuver. For a few seconds, it looked as though the two sets of vessels would clash head-on.

Then Arany's ships ducked. There was no better word for it. The dive beneath the flight path of the fighters was a deliberate evasion. The fighters flew over the top of the freeships and Carosa heard the coordinators screaming instructions to flip and chase, rotate, *rotate*, damn it!

Pramoda stared at the screen with the same degree of curiosity as Carosa. "I do believe they mean to attack. Us, I mean." He glanced at Carosa. "The fighters will easily catch them. The freeships are not nearly fast enough to outrun them."

Carosa frowned. Had he missed something? What had he overlooked? He didn't underestimate Arany. The man had caused more than casual damage to over a dozen naval vessels. He had to know that sprinting toward a cruiser was a fast form of suicide.

He sat up as alarm bloomed hot in his chest and guts. "Get the forcefields up! Now!"

Pramoda passed on the order, then looked at Carosa, baffled. "The fighters will take care of them."

"All of them? Before they reach us?" Carosa snapped coldly.

"Enough of them to make the rest not matter."

Carosa shook his head. "Get us out of here, Pramoda. Null jump. I don't care where. Just do it."

"Sir, the fighters…"

"We'll come back and pick them up, if there are any left." Carosa slapped the arm of his chair. "*Now!*"

Heads snapped around to look at him.

"Fighters engaged!" the mid-shipman called.

Pramoda frowned down at his bench. "We will be able to jump in sixty seconds."

Carosa slumped back. "Too long." He looked at the screen. The fighters were firing at the backs of the freeships. Carosa had seen the fighters do the same with Karassian units. Usually, the ships that were struck bloomed into an instant fireball, that evaporated immediately. A split-second marker of death.

He could see the freeships taking hits. Two of them stopped dead in space. Yet none of them flared into flames.

"They're all shielded," Pramoda breathed. His tone said he finally understood. "They're slower, because they're shielded."

Carosa watched the screen.

"They still can't touch us," Pramoda added. "The fields are in place. The limited ammunition they have can't get through."

Carosa watched the freeship squad draw closer, dread pooling at the pit of his stomach. "Send for assistance." He couldn't raise his voice.

"Sir!" Pramoda protested.

"Do it." Carosa looked back at the screen, at the approaching ships.

Pramoda sent the communications bullet then looked up again. "They're going to have to break off their approach soon, or they'll…" Carosa heard his quick intake of breath.

The freeships grew enormous on the screen. The scanners zoomed back, but couldn't retract fast enough. The last thing Captain Carosa saw was the bellies of dozens of ships as all but one of them skimmed over the top of the *Jovian*. One of the freighters ploughed straight ahead, ramming through forcefields designed to repel light and heat, slicing through hull and superstructure. The freeships were slow compared to the fighters, although that was relative. The freighter hit the side of the *Jovian* at thousands of kilometers an hour. It wasn't a collision, for the freighter instantly detonated, spewing active fuel into the *Jovian*, while the splinters and fragments of the ship tore through multiple decks, destabilizing structures, destroying bulkheads and killing crewmembers just as they recognized the danger.

The screens were blank, although Carosa, who had been recruited into the Navy because of his astro-physics education, could tell what had happened through the shuddering and flexing of the deck beneath his feet and the rumbling that quickly rose in volume to become a roar.

"They flew into us!" Pramoda cried, gripping the bench in front of him for stability. "Sir, the damage...!"

"Destruction, Pramoda," Carosa said calmly. "They've killed us."

#

Pleasure Dome, Antini III, Free Space.

The news of the destruction of the *Jovian* by a little group of freeships sent a frisson of shock through the known worlds. It was as if everyone paused to draw a breath and re-orient themselves in the face of a game-changing disaster.

"Of course, here on Antini, we take no notice of the war at all, as you can see," the nearly naked host explained to them, as he—or she—Reynard Cardenas could not determine, led the small party through the public areas of the dome. "We are at capacity right now and have been since the disaster." The host smiled at them, showing dimples. "If not for your very special hosts insisting upon accommodations, we might not have been able to find the space you need."

The public areas were just that—a series of areas designed to resemble other world locations. They had crossed romantic bridges over slow-flowing streams, moved across parkland, followed a trail through a dense woodland and walked along a planked sidewalk next to a sandy beach. It wasn't the areas that sent shock slithering through Reynard's veins. It was the uninhibited sexual activity that was taking place in any direction he turned his gaze. Inside the punt meandering along the slow river, on the sandy beach, on the bridge itself as they squeezed past, people were coupling in fevered twos, threes and more. It wasn't just people, either. There were animals and biobots, even metal help-meets that had been enhanced with genitals — an aberration that made Reynard moan in disgust.

After a few minutes of the orgasmic excess, Reynard grew inured to the effect. He trod steadily after the host, his men around him, and kept his gaze on the host's back.

There was a little house just ahead, with quaint windows that opened and closed and a door with a round handle. The host turned the handle and pushed the door open, then stepped aside. "Enjoy your meeting, gentlemen." He/she smiled widely.

Gaubert gripped his arm. "Let me go first." He stepped inside, the top of his head brushing the doorframe.

Reynard ducked under the frame and followed him.

The inside of the house was quite innocent. Everything seemed to be inanimate and simple. The flooring was soft. Reynard realized why the floor was a spongy texture and grimaced again.

A round table was sitting in the middle of the room beyond the door. There were five people sitting around the far side of it, just as there were five men in Reynard's group. All of those sitting had the blond hair and brown eyes of the standard Karassian. One of the men already seated was half-cyborg. His arms were robotic, so was his neck. Reynard had to force himself not to stare.

The man in the middle, though, looked perfectly normal. Reynard wondered if he was as purely human as he appeared. The walk through the Pleasure Dome had reminded Reynard that beyond the borders of Erium, transhumans were common and accepted as equals. He glared at the man in the middle. "Did you insist upon meeting here to remind us of our loss, Woodrow?"

Woodrow spread his hands, his round face breaking into a smile. "We prefer that you be reminded by this place that cooperation is possible even amongst those with nothing in common."

"I consider myself reminded." Reynard did not sit down. "You asked for this meeting. I suggest you get to the point. I do not bargain well when I am nauseous."

Woodrow raised his brows. "We are not here to bargain. Oh, dear. I must apologize if that is the impression you were given. Sit, Cardenas. We, the Karassian people, have a gift for you."

Reynard stayed on his feet. "Why would a Karassian want to give me a gift?"

"We are all empathetic beings, are we not?"

Reynard didn't bother responding.

Woodrow's smile faded. "Your family in particular has felt the bite of free state violence lately. I understand that the captain of the *Jovian* was a first cousin of yours. And of course, the murder of your son, only meters away from where we sit…"

Reynard made an impatient gesture. "Your point, Woodrow?"

"No one knows who murdered your son. Perhaps we'll never know. However, the party responsible for the destruction of the *Jovian*…well, that is different."

"You speak of Benjamin Arany and his fleet as if your intelligence corps has uncovered a great secret. We have known about Arany for years."

"Yes, but do you know where his base of operations is located?" Woodrow asked. His smile returned. "Not even your much vaunted intelligence machine has been able to find that out, has it?" Woodrow put his hand on the shoulder of the small, pale man with red-shot eyes, who sat next to him.

Reynard let his gaze flicker over the man and an atavistic shiver rippled over him. He would arrange to never be alone with that one. True madness shone from his eyes.

"This is Ferid, who is *not* part of the Karassian Intelligence Corps, so if you think to waylay him later and pump him for information about Karassian affairs you would be wasting your time." Woodrow lowered his hand, while Ferid gave a smile that was chilling in its good cheer.

"Ferid has learned the location of Arany's fleet, where they hide out when not destroying Eriuman cruisers," Woodrow said.

Gaubert turned so his shoulder was to the table and spoke urgently. "You cannot accept this information, Reynard. It will be tainted. The Karassians do not hand over gifts like this without a price."

Reynard barely heard him. There was a high note singing in his mind, making thought difficult, except for one shining concept.

Vengeance.

Gaubert gripped his forearm and squeezed hard. "Death is the price of war. Sher Corvosa knew that as thoroughly as Max did. This would not be war."

"Let me go," Reynard said, not bothering to lower his voice. Over Gaubert's shoulder, he could see Ferid's grin and Woodrow watching with close scrutiny.

"You would dishonor their deaths," Gaubert said, his voice low.

Reynard looked at him. "Max was dismembered and disemboweled, here, in this place. What honor was there in that?"

"You would seek vengeance for his death by treating with these people?" Gaubert asked. He glanced over his shoulder. "They *want* you to take the information. For that reason alone, you should refuse it. We can find Arany for ourselves if you really want his blood to spill."

Reynard breathed out the miasma that choked his throat. He looked at Gaubert. "I really want it." And he closed his eyes. "Just not this way," he added softly. "Clean. Swift. Untainted. Merciless. That is what I want."

Gaubert gripped his arm. "Go back to the shuttle. I'll send these Karassians on their way. Go on."

Reynard sucked in the warm air. It was difficult to breathe here. He suddenly longed for the hills of Cardenas and the cool air there. Even if the house was silent these days, it was his. He was an outsider here. So he nodded at Gaubert and turned and left. He did not miss the startled expressions of the Karassians and took a pinch of comfort in defying their expectations. He was Eriuman. It was good to be unpredictable.

#

When his older brother had left, the door of the house clicking shut behind him, Gaubert turned back to Woodrow and leaned over the table. "I am not my brother," he said, speaking quickly. "He would destroy your enemy for personal vengeance. I would do it for Erium. Tell me where to find Arany."

Chapter Fifteen

Cardenas (Findlay IV), Findlay System, Eriuman Republic.

Khalil used the last of his liquid currency to pay the shuttle to put him down just outside the town. There was no issue finding a suitably flat and supportive place to land. The earth in every direction was a blasted plane of dried out earth, cracked and devoid of plant life.

The sun was blazing overhead, heat haze making it look as though it was throbbing.

The shuttle pilot glanced around as the port door opened, then tossed Khalil a canteen. The contents sloshed. The canteen was heavy. "You're going to need it," the pilot said.

Khalil gave his thanks and stepped out onto the earth, which disintegrated under the weight of his foot. Dust rose up around his boot. He pulled the hood of his jacket up over his head, as protection against the sun and started walking toward the black smudge on the horizon where the town lay.

As soon as he was out of range, the pilot took off. The shuttle rocketed upward. Khalil didn't look back.

After two kilometers, Khalil reconsidered how much farther he had to go. Distance was deceptive here. The town was no closer and he had already drained the canteen. The heat was intolerable, beating up at him from the ground and wafting around him as he moved through the warm air. The sun was almost directly overhead and he could feel the flesh on the back of his hands burning. He took the warning to heart and did not lower the hood.

He walked, even though his pace slowed. There was no other choice.

After another kilometer he paused to catch his breath. The smudge on the horizon was larger. There was regular shaping to its edges, suggesting buildings or other structures. Also, a plume of smoke was rising from it.

Khalil blinked, trying to make his eyes focus properly.

It wasn't smoke. It was a pillar of sand. Something was kicking up the very fine dirt, flinging it into the air where it rose like smoke into the very pale blue sky. The something was heading his way.

Khalil started walking again, taking inventory of the possessions distributed around his body and clothes. Some had barter value.

The plume grew closer and now he could see the progress of the vehicle that was making it. It looked as though it was moving fast, yet it would still take minutes to reach him. As it drew closer, he could see more detail and realized there were two vehicles.

When they were close enough for him to hear the engines, he stopped. They should surely be able to see him with the naked eye, now. Their path toward him had been direct, which meant they had tracked him by some type of scanner, possibly from the moment he stepped off the shuttle. Or earlier.

That spoke of a level of sophistication in technology that didn't match the little town Khalil had spotted from high orbit.

The two vehicles stopped on either side of him and seven men jumped out. They were typical Eriumans.

One of them, with long hair pinned to his shoulder, faced him. "You should have stayed on your ship," he said, showing bad teeth.

"I'm here to speak to Bellona."

The man smiled, revealing more stumps. "Get lost, did you? Your shiny ship not have a compass?"

"I know she is here. Give her my name. She will speak to me." In fact, he wasn't entirely sure if his name would have any effect at all, but these were low-level, unimaginative people. He had to get past them before reasoning would work.

The spokesman shook his head. "You're in the wrong place at the wrong time, my friend. Go home. It's safer there."

Khalil stepped back as the others moved forward. Hands gripped his arms and Khalil sighed. Clearly, these men had not been trained by Bellona. It took little effort to drop them all. They were almost comically predictable. While he was dealing with the sixth, he pulled his knife from the hidden pocket. He tossed the deadweight of the sixth into the shocked arms of the spokesman and came up behind it. He got the knife under Bad Teeth's ear and let it prick the skin there, enough for the man to feel the sting.

Bad Teeth yipped in reaction.

As the others stirred sluggishly around them, Khalil walked the man to one of the cars and forced him behind the controls. Khalil sat behind him. "Take me to Abilio."

"They'll kill you," Bad Teeth said, trying to roll his eyes to look at Khalil over his shoulder, without puncturing himself on the end of Khalil's knife.

"I'll take that risk," Khalil said honestly.

"Oh, he's going to grind you to paste," Bad Teeth added, starting up the car. "I really hope I get to see it."

#

The remaining few kilometers into the little town took mere minutes, compared to the slow pace of the first four. Khalil resisted the temptation to let his hood drop and his sweaty face cool in the breeze created by the motion of the car. The sun was still overhead and still dazzling. The crew of seven who had been sent to deal with him all wore hats and long sleeved shirts. Besides, if there had been one spy satellite trained on this place, then there could be more. Better to remain a white blob on any feeds.

The town was as lonely and decrepit as it had appeared from space. Down on the ground, though, the smell of dust and decay made it very real. The main road through the little town was dirt. There were imprints in the surface where a heavy vehicle had driven over the dirt while it was wet. The tread marks were still sharp, even though the last rains had been weeks ago. Very few vehicles had passed over the top of them to wear them down.

No one walked the streets or peered out of windows as they passed the handful of buildings. All the buildings were of the old design, with four walls, windows and doors, which served well in remote locations. None of these had seen any maintenance for many years. Dust clung to everything, making every building look brown and drab.

There was an even older and more ramshackle shed ahead, with half a kilometer separating it from the town itself. One of the walls had collapsed inward. The lack of support made the roof sag in the middle, along the length of the missing wall. It looked as though a good breeze would knock down the lot.

Bad Teeth steered the car through the leaning door, into the shed and halted.

"Now where?" Khalil demanded, getting out.

Bad Teeth shrugged. "We wait."

"I said I wanted to speak to Bellona."

"You speak to my boss first. If you're lucky, he'll pass you through. If you're not..." Bad Teeth grinned. "I hope you're not."

"How long do we wait? Is there a signal?"

"He knows we're here already. He's a busy man, though."

Khalil weighed up his options. It was more than likely that Bad Teeth really did not know where to go beyond this point, which gave him an indirect hope. If they were operating with cut-offs like this, insulating themselves, that was a good sign.

He motioned Bad Teeth out from behind the controls. He didn't want the man taking off if his attention slipped. He pulled him over to the shadiest corner and pushed him down into it. Then he sat with his back against the raw mudbrick wall.

It was after dark before anyone came. By then, both of them were freezing. Abilio was on a desert plain at a high altitude and close to the equator. Once the direct, glaring sun had gone down, the heat left the day and the true coolness of the altitude could be felt.

Bad Teeth was as miserable as Khalil and made no attempt to unwrap his arms from around his legs and escape. Khalil hunched over his knees and tried to stop his teeth from chattering. He needed to hear if anyone approached.

When they did arrive, it was with complete silence. They were a dark shape that detached itself from the deeper shadows and loomed up over the two of them. A short man, wrapped in a warm cloak and hood.

Khalil scrambled to get up, alarm moving sluggishly through him. He gripped the knife with his cold fingers.

A hand shot out of the dark cloak and gripped his wrist. "There is no need for that." The voice was a musical tenor. The fingers were strong around his wrist, squeezing the tendons to weaken his grip. The man reached up to drop the hood back.

"Sang," Khalil breathed, shock slithering through him. "Stars and moons...Sang!"

Sang was undoubtedly a man. There was stubble on his cheeks, the same coppery blond as his hair, which was trimmed short. In the dark, Khalil could not see if the freckles that had highlighted Sang's face before were still there. The fine jaw and chin seemed stronger.

"Khalil Ready," Sang said. "You have risked much to reach this far."

Khalil saw Sang's laryngeal peak shift at the front of his throat as he spoke. It was fascinating to watch simply because it had never been there before. "In truth, there has been little risk so far." He looked down at Bad Teeth, who was still shivering in the corner, too miserable to care about anything else. "They were not trained."

Sang smiled. "We spend a lot of money keeping people away from here without raising suspicions."

"Money can be neutralized by even more money." Khalil put the knife away. "I need to see her, Sang. It's important."

Sang didn't move. "How did you find us?"

Khalil shrugged. "The same way I found you on Kachmar. Bellona cannot move off this planet without someone noticing. Xenia is too well known. As no one has shouted about seeing her, she had to be here, still. Clearly, she is not in the city anymore…" He paused, remembering his surprise when he saw Bellona was not on the family dais, marking Max's passing. "After that, it was a matter of analyzing satellite feeds and extrapolating."

Sang sighed. "There is one independent satellite I cannot control. The AI is anti-social and incorruptible. It limits everything we do here."

"That is most likely the feed I accessed," Khalil told him. "It was the absence of people, Sang. You should do something about that."

"There are empty towns all over the desert," Sang pointed out.

"None of them have tire tracks as this one does."

Sang weighed up his observation, his strange pale eyes focused on nothing. "It is a risk, but there are few people with the skills to sweet-talk the satellite and fewer with reason to look so closely in the first place." He took Khalil's arm. "Come. How does a warm room, mulled wine and hot cakes sound?"

"Glorious," Khalil admitted.

Sang walked him back out of the rickety shed and into the night. The air beyond the walls was even more frigid than inside and Khalil shivered again.

"You've come from warmer places," Sang observed.

"I would have called this place warm, today."

Sang smiled. "The extremes of temperature test everything, here. People. Metal and plastics. Compounds that survive the vacuum of space will crack through the middle overnight here." He was heading in the direction of the nearest ramshackle building. "Humans have been living on Cardenas for over seven hundred years, yet they have never been able to live in the Caramella desert for long. Plants shrivel. Water evaporates, or freezes and shatters whatever contains it, then is lost the next day when it melts." He paused with his foot on the flat, broad step beneath the door, which looked as though it was hanging by one hinge only. He breathed out heavily. The air clouded in front of his mouth. "Not long after midnight, it will drop to two hundred and fifty kays." He pushed open the door, which swung in silently. It was still and dark in the room beyond. Khalil stepped in cautiously. It didn't seem to be much warmer than outside, either.

Sang shut the door. From the inside, it closed with a firm click. Then Sang pushed Khalil toward the back of the room and placed his hand on the wall next to him.

A disguised palm pad.

The floor in the middle of the room descended, leaving a gaping rectangle of shadow.

"The light will improve as you descend," Sang said. "After you."

Khalil groped with his boot for the first step and took it cautiously. Then the next. The stairs were sound and even, which gave him the courage to continue down into the blackness. As soon as his head was beneath the level of the floor above, he spotted tiny pilot lights ahead, each of them outlining a single step and no farther. There were dozens of them, disappearing down even deeper.

"Underground," he muttered. "It is completely obvious, in hindsight."

"As long as it remains obvious only in hindsight, our security holds," Sang murmured, from right behind him.

As they descended, the air around them grew warmer. Khalil heard the floor of the old building above them move back into place. He descended, one step after another, the little lights guiding the way. On either side was what looked like rock face. It had been burned away with cutters. The face of it gleamed like black glass.

There was stronger light farther ahead and a murmur of sound. The air was definitely warmer now and blew gently against Khalil's face. He pushed the hood back gratefully. The flesh over his cheekbones relaxed, telling him the air down here carried more moisture than the air over the desert, above. Somewhere, there was water.

The stairs ended and the walls opened out into a small room with three sealed doors. The door directly ahead of the stairs was the one from where the noise was coming. Sang, though, opened the door on the right. There was another room beyond.

"Come in," Sang said.

Khalil stepped into the room and looked around curiously. There was a colorful rug on the floor. A comfortable chair and a small table and a cupboard were the only pieces of furniture, although there was barely room for any more.

"Cozy," Khalil remarked.

"Have a seat," Sang said. He stepped over to the cupboard, opened it, reached in and withdrew a tray holding a samovar and a plate of steaming hot cakes. He carried the tray over to the little table.

Khalil sat in the chair. It was soft and deep and he arranged himself so his weight was at the front of the cushion. "Bad Teeth…the man who brought me here, the one we left in the shed. He said you would take a while because you're busy."

Sang smiled. "I am."

"That isn't why you took so long, though. You were waiting to see if anyone was following me."

Sang poured the mulled wine into the short, wide cup sitting on the tray and handed it to him. "Drink."

Khalil took the cup. "Clearly, no one was, or I wouldn't be here. Only, now we're sitting in this room that doesn't seem to have a purpose and isn't connected to anything. What are you waiting for this time?"

Sang stood back. "The scans are unobtrusive. The questions…well, they are a little more direct."

Khalil smiled. "You have never been anything *but* direct." He sipped. The mulled wine was as good as any he had ever tasted in the Cardenas homebase. "Ask, Sang. I will answer."

Sang nodded. "Why are you here?"

"To speak to Bellona."

"So you said." Sang considered him. "Why do you want to speak to Bellona?"

Khalil weighed up his options. If he refused to answer, Sang would stonewall him. Khalil had seen him endlessly prevaricate over allowing strangers access to the homebase in the city. He would stay calm and absolutely unmoving, until Khalil wore himself out.

On the other hand, Khalil had no doubts about Sang's loyalty to Bellona. He wondered if Bellona had learned to trust him yet.

Khalil relaxed. "Are the scans done?"

Sang considered. "Yes."

"There is no chance of being overheard, here?"

"That is why I brought you to this room in particular."

Khalil nodded. "I know who killed Max."

Chapter Sixteen

Cardenas (Findlay IV), Findlay System, Eriuman Republic

On the other side of the door from where all the noise had been seeping was a cavern, buzzing with industry and people. The door had been close to soundproof, so the volume that leapt when Sang pushed open the door startled Khalil.

The place may have started as a cave, once upon a time, although that simple description had been left behind. The same cutters that had made the stair walls smooth and strong had carved out a cavern with high vertical walls and a flat roof far overhead. Pillars of native rock had been carved in place and these had been used to divide the open cavern into areas of use.

Somewhere unseen, farther back in the cavern, metal was being hammered. Machinery hummed, engines roared, punctuated by pneumatic hisses. This, then, was the engineering section.

Sang touched Khalil's shoulder, drawing his attention, then beckoned. Sang moved along the side of the cavern, where a path had been left clear. People were using the path, farther ahead, to traverse the cavern, then stepping off the path into the section they wanted.

Of the many people walking about the cavern that Khalil could see, going about their mysterious business, only about half of them were native Eriumans. There were many people with undefined genetic markers, which meant they were most likely free staters.

Khalil's curiosity rose. What was she doing?

Farther along the wide path, there was an open area, where people were training. Khalil recognized the movements as pure Bellona-Xenia style combat, but Bellona was not there. The instructor lifted a hand in acknowledgement when she saw Sang and Khalil. Sang waved back.

The training area was well lit by the daylights blazing from the adjacent area. Long rows of waist-high benches held green, growing things. Food for the workers, that could not grow on the surface. Robot gardeners rolled up and down the rows, tending the plants.

The end of the long cavern was on the other side of the greenhouse, while the path continued, burrowing through a door-shaped hole in the wall and turning into a tunnel.

The noise dropped.

"How many people are here?" Khalil asked, catching up with Sang.

Sang glanced at him and shook his head. "You know I can't tell you that."

So. He had been granted a qualified access. For now, it would do. Khalil contented himself with keeping his eyes open, instead.

The tunnel was featureless and long. There were doors on the right-hand side only and few of them. Khalil kept count.

Sang stopped at one of the doors and put his hand to the wall. The door opened and Sang waved him ahead once more.

This room was larger, yet just as plain and simple. It had two other doors, one to the right and one to the left. Sang shut the main door behind them and moved over to the right -hand door and tapped on it.

"In a minute, Sang!"

Khalil drew a breath. It was Bellona's voice.

There were no chairs in the room. No desks, no furniture that hinted at the use of the room. There was a single cupboard and there was a samovar and cups sitting on it. Steam rose from the spout of the samovar.

Sang poured a cup of the wine and gave it to Khalil. "I whisked you away from your last cup. This will take the cold from your bones."

The door opened and Bellona moved into the room. She looked as though she was a match for this place. The boots and pants and workman-like shirt were appropriate. The ghostmaker on her hip looked natural. Her gaze came to rest on Khalil. "Was he scanned, Sang?"

"He has a knife in his right boot and a miniature ghost-maker in his pocket. I didn't bother removing them."

Bellona glanced at Sang. "You would rather watch me have to do that?"

"Very much so," Sang said with relish. "You would not be gentle, if he tried to use them."

Khalil sighed. "I am here on peaceful business."

"Not if you are here to dangle my brother's killer in front of me," Bellona replied. She crossed her arms.

Khalil put the cup back on the cupboard. "I could give you the name of the responsible party, but you would not believe me. So I must pave the way. Would you indulge me that much time?"

"I don't have the time to spare that you would need to redeem yourself," Bellona said.

"I am not here for that," Khalil said shortly. "I merely need you to believe me when I tell you the name. To do that, I must account for myself since I left Cardenas."

Sang smiled. "You joined your brother, Benjamin Arany, on the *Bonaventura*. You have been there ever since."

Khalil didn't bother hiding his surprise. "You've been tracking me, Sang?"

"Then Sang was right," Bellona said slowly. "You didn't go back to the Bureau."

Khalil spread his hands. "I told you I was done with them."

Bellona remained silent and still. The stillness was a new quality. She was holding everything inside her. Weighing it for herself, instead of spilling her emotions about like a fountain.

"Go on," she said at last.

"Last month, I met a bureau field agent on Laurasia. It was a purely accidental meeting. It was also an awkward one. He spoke much and said very little, and looked longingly toward the door in between. There was one thing he said, though, that stayed with me."

Both Sang and Bellona were watching him carefully, assessing every word. They did not interrupt with questions.

"He said the prostitutes were prettier on Laurasia."

Sang's eyes narrowed.

Bellona touched Sang's arm, as if she had felt his sudden attention. Then she looked at Khalil. "His name?"

"He wouldn't have travelled under that name."

"You know what aliases he uses?" Sang asked, using the remote, unmodulated tone that said he was thinking digitally, tapping into networks and sifting data.

Khalil gave them. "I have already tracked them as far as I can," he added.

Bellona's smile was small. "Sang and Connie can track more between them. You knew that. That's why you're here."

Khalil held his jaw together. Then he frowned. "Who is Connie?"

"You know her. It. The AI in the Karassian yacht that Sang bought to Kachmar."

Sang was standing perfectly still, staring at nothing.

"*She*?" Khalil said.

"I call her that," Bellona said. "It makes things easier."

"Isn't the yacht impounded by the Navy, somewhere

over the city?"

"Which is why she's bored. Connie likes to talk to Sang."

Khalil considered that. "Connie is a Karassian."

"She's an AI with limited experience," Sang said, his voice as remote as his gaze. "She is a child. A gifted one with access to data pools I could not reach myself. War is a concept she has not yet grasped." He frowned. "This is getting interesting…" he murmured.

Bellona moved away from Sang and gestured for Khalil to shift over to the far side of the room with her. They stood next to the samovar.

"You already know where this trail will end, don't you?" she asked him.

Khalil sighed. "If I'm right, then the trail will end on Antini. So will one or two other Bureau people's trails."

Bellona was still showing no emotion. "The Bureau killed Max? Why?"

"I don't know for sure, although I do know how they work. Do you remember when I told you about their search for a hero?"

"Isn't Arany the hero they've been waiting for?" Bellona asked. "He's a leader, visible, committed…"

Khalil nodded. "There were hundreds of potential candidates. Ben was one, yes. So was Xenia. I thought I had convinced the Bureau that you were not a viable possibility anymore. Xenia had gone." He spread his hands. "What if they didn't believe me?"

"What would they do if they dismissed your analysis?"

"They would have Ben, they would have you, and who knows how many others. The Bureau likes to work with certainties whenever they can arrange them, to offset the statistical predictions they play with most of the time. Every analysis and projection they have run in the last two generations has pointed toward the emergence of a leader, someone who would massively impact the known worlds, who would institute change at a level a simple war would never achieve. If the Bureau itself is to survive that upheaval, then they would have to identify the hero as early as possible and find a way to stay within their sphere of influence." Khalil met her gaze. "Maybe they wanted to force the issue."

"By making *their* choice the hero?" Bellona frowned. "Could they do that? Would they?"

Khalil grimaced. "I've seen them arrange matters to suit themselves. In the past, the changes they made were benign. A nudge here, a tweak there, for a more favorable outcome. I've seen them buy stocks, rig votes, sully reputations…it was all minor and the outcome was always positive…"

"Until now," Bellona finished.

Khalil rubbed his temples. He'd had little sleep in the last week of frantic, extended travel. On top of his exhaustion, even considering what he was about to say made him feel ill. "You were entrenched in your family's homebase, Bellona. Xenia was disappearing from the public's memory. Your father was boxing you in with suitors and expectations. What if the Bureau…" He swallowed. "What if they decided to change that? A hero needs pressure to emerge. What if they added that pressure? Say, by slipping your father a discrediting file about me, to get me out of the picture? Then, by murdering the one ally you had left in the city?"

"Max," Bellona breathed. Anger grew in her eyes. "Only, I came here," she said flatly.

Khalil nodded. "Proving that the pressure wasn't quite enough yet for you to pick up even a metaphorical sword. However, if they let you know how you'd been manipulated, say, by giving me just enough information to start me down the path to the truth…?"

Bellona's lips parted. "They're manipulating you, too."

"I think so, yes. That's how profoundly elegant their plan is. It doesn't matter if I know. I would have come here, anyway. The fact alone was enough to push me into this." He sighed. "I had no choice but to tell you. They knew it."

Bellona looked at him for a long, silent moment. Then, without turning her head, she said, "Sang?"

"Still confirming, although it is looking more likely by the minute," Sang said.

Bellona nodded. "Come with me," she told Khalil. "I have something to show you."

#

At the far end of the passage, there were two openings. One was a rough hole in the rock face. From farther inside the hole the hum of drilling equipment could be heard. Bright work lights shone deep inside the burrow.

Bellona nodded toward the burrow. "There is a huge water basin a hundred meters below us. The water filters down from the surface. On the way through it leaves behind minerals and salt. The money we raise from exporting them gives us the raw materials we can't produce ourselves, although we're very close to self-sufficient here. The holes left behind by the mining become new living spaces." As she spoke, she palmed a pad next to the other door, then tapped out a pattern.

The door unsealed with loud thud of solid locks shifting.

"You developed all this yourself?"

"There was already a mine operating when Sang and I got here, although it was a sporadic and badly organized operation. Sang sorted out the operation while I convinced the miners that my way would be better."

"And your way is what, exactly?"

Bellona pushed on the door and it opened with the slowness of an airlock door moving on sluggish hinges. As it opened, lights came on in the area beyond.

Bellona stepped over the sill and held the door open for Khalil. He followed her in.

It was another large cavern, at least as long as the passage on the other side of the wall, which explained why there were no doors on the left side. The cavern was wider than it was long, creating a floor space of at least several hectares.

Despite the size, the whole cavern was taken up by a single ship, sitting silently in the middle, with its boarding ramps down.

Khalil sucked in a shocked breath. "That's a Karassian frigate…"

Bellona crossed her arms. "It's a full scale replica. You could punch your fist through the bulkheads if you wanted to. The layout inside is identical to the real thing, though. It took us months to build it, but we had to have it for training purposes."

Khalil thought of the people he had seen on the way in, completing personal combat exercises. "Training for what?" he asked. "Why would you want a mock-up of a Karassian ship, unless…" He turned to look at her for confirmation. "You're going to steal one."

She smiled. "We are."

Khalil walked over to the ship. It was huge, the blunt nose sitting many meters above his head. "The only reason to need a Karassian ship is because you intend to travel through Karassian space and don't want to be waylaid, or even noticed."

"That is certainly the ideal, but that is not the ultimate reason for stealing a Karassian ship." Bellona walked over to the nearest boarding ramp and put her hand on the support strut. "With this, we can get down on the surface, unquestioned."

Khalil thought it through. "Using the ship's own registration to get past sentries?"

She nodded.

"Where are you going?"

"Kachmar."

Khalil drew in a sharp, surprised breath. "You're going back to Ledan."

Bellona looked up at the belly of the ship. "I'm going to get them all out, Ari. Every single one of them."

His heart gave a little squeeze at the name. Flashes of memory, of times that only *seemed* peaceful and content, flickered through his mind, barely seen, although they provoked the anger, anyway. Even though he had known what Appurtenance Services Inc would do to him, the sense of betrayal had been huge. He had used his outrage to free her from that place. Bellona had been held inside the dream for ten years. Her anger was so much greater than his could ever be.

"You don't want them to be lied to anymore," Khalil said.

Bellona's smile was warm. "I knew you would understand." Her smile grew. "As you can see, I'm picking up the sword."

He moved away from the nose, back toward the door, where he could see all of the ship at once. "So you steal the ship, land on Ledania, take everyone off with the help of your mining friends...then what, Bellona?"

"Once everyone is out of that place, then I will tell the known worlds what the Karassians have done. I will stand next to my friends and we will expose the Homogeny as the monster it really is."

"And then what?"

Her smile faded. "One step at a time."

"You don't know. You haven't thought beyond releasing them and exposing Karassia."

"Isn't that enough? I'm not your Bureau's hero, Khalil."

"And if you learn that the Bureau really did kill Max?"

"Then I will have my next step."

"Even if you are doing exactly what the Bureau want you to do?"

She considered that. "It appears I will have as little choice as you. I will have to act, even knowing that is what they want."

"So, first Karassia, then the Bureau. What then of Erium?"

Her brows came together. "Erium has done nothing but defend itself."

"Your father and your family are the perfect representatives of Erium. Look at what they did to you. Look at where you stand. Can you still say truthfully they have done nothing?"

"It is I who no longer fits Erium. It isn't their fault. They behaved naturally, which collided with my differences, that is all." She came closer. "What is it that you want of me, Khalil? You want me to be the hero the Bureau are searching for? You want me to take on everyone, even Erium?"

"I want you to see yourself for what you really are."

"What am I?"

"You think you are a lost soul in search of meaning. I see a leader rescuing her tribe."

"Yet you told the Bureau I was not one, that Xenia had gone."

"Xenia *is* gone," Khalil said. "Although that was the only truthful thing I told them."

Bellona turned away, hiding her reaction. She kept her back to him. "I accept none of it," she told him. Her voice was strained. "I'm not a hero. I'm not even a leader. I just want to help my friends. That's all."

"Very well," Khalil replied. "If you would permit, I would like to help you with that. They were my friends, too."

She glanced over her shoulder. There was a pleased expression in her eyes. "If you do, you will be declaring your loyalties for the worlds to see. Your brother…"

"Will understand," Khalil said. "We two have walked different paths since we were taken off Revati and he was given to a family on Cerce, while I remained on Atticus."

"You won't be able to cling to the shadows the way the Bureau does, not after this."

"Every step I've taken since I woke up in that Kachmarain gutter has led to this," Khalil said. He tried to sound calm, even though his heart was racing. "This is *my* next step."

Chapter Seventeen

Cardenas (Findlay IV), Findlay System, Eriuman Republic.

Sang quickly grew used to hearing soft, easy chatter in Bellona's suite, once Khalil returned. Because Sang oversaw every aspect of the colony, he knew that Khalil took one of the tiny sitting rooms in the old section as his quarters and he returned to them every night. At most other times, though, Khalil could be found in the center room, applying his ability to think in structures and systems to Bellona's plans.

Sang was included in the free-flow, long discussions where most of the final decisions were made. He took care of implementing them.

The center room, which had once been devoid of anything useful, became a gathering room. Chairs were grown, a small table appeared. None of them matched. Cushion colors clashed. Yet the chairs were comfortable and the table useful. Possessions littered horizontal surfaces, giving the room an untidy, lived-in appearance. Sang found the clutter odd after the disciplined simplicity of the Cardenas family home, but not unpleasant.

Sang also spent time maintaining the relationship he had

built with Connie, as the AI had wanted be called. Bellona called Connie "she" because of the feminine tag, yet Sang could discern no gender in the AI and barely any personality beyond that of an unformed, mostly bewildered child. Previous owners of the yacht had not interfaced with the AI except with direct commands. Connie had been socially retarded when Sang had reached out to the yacht. However, Connie would be instrumental in their plans for Ledan, so Sang liked to keep her placid and happy by off-setting the first tendrils of loneliness she was beginning to experience.

Khalil reviewed the already-made decisions with Sang, too. "Which came first?" he asked Sang. "A convenient desert where a Karassian frigate can be landed, or the lack of satellite coverage except for one that you control?"

Sang shook his head. "I don't control it. Not yet."

"Controlling it and limiting it would set off alarm signals, of course."

"When landing guidance is needed, will be soon enough to sever its strings."

Khalil pursed his full lips. "The timing will be critical."

"Every element of this venture is critical. We are heading into the heart of Karassian territory, to an installation that has been raided once already. The Karassians have many faults, yet they are very good at learning from experience. We won't be able to stroll into the compound the way we did last time." Sang paused. "My timing will be accurate," he added.

"If we had not strolled into the compound the first time, there would be no driving force for the second. It is what it is."

Bellona's driving force was considerable. "My memories of Ledan are of kinder people, all of them open-hearted, with no agendas and no expectations," she had explained. "It angers me to think of them being manipulated as they are."

"They will not be like that once they remember who they are," Khalil warned her.

"We all are like that, inside."

"No," Khalil said firmly. "There are monsters parading as humans. You could dig to their centers and fail to find that core."

"No one in Ledan is like that," Bellona said. "Their cores were exposed, there. Enhanced, biobots, cybernetics, freaks all of them, but human, at the base."

"You trust them," Sang surmised.

"More than anyone in the known worlds," Bellona said.

Khalil remained silent. Yet he did not look away. His posture did not shift. He had already accepted this truth, then. He understood his position with a clarity that was rare among humans.

Sang knew Khalil's complacency wouldn't last. No one, not even Sang, could live with qualified acceptance in the long term. Belonging was a basic human drive that androids, whose awareness was patterned upon human awareness, and AIs, who aped human consciousness, also shared.

As it turned out, it wasn't just Khalil who was blasted out of stasis.

#

The news came from every shaded source Sang had, including Connie, who babbled in panic as she was a Karassian ship in Eriuman space. The satellite also reported high yield news streams, while the data pools within which Sang kept a mental taprod all shivered with the impact.

The known worlds bolted upright, the trivia of the everyday evaporating, as they measured their neighbors, terrified.

Sang absorbed the baseline facts as he ran for Bellona's quarters. By the time he pushed on the heavy door and stepped inside, he had assembled it into shocking whole.

Bellona and Khalil were talking to Shalev Zeni. Zeni was responsible for the personal combat readiness of everyone who would be going to Kachmar. Her work was made difficult because of the cultural bias of the known worlds: Big ships did the fighting.

Overcoming resistance to learning self-defense was a constant topic with Zeni. Bellona was sanguine, though. "When they face their first test of physical strength and readiness, they will either die, or they will understand. I don't care which. It is up to them. I, though, intend to survive."

Bellona trained harder than anyone else in the caverns except for Khalil, who had already faced reality at least once. Her example and Khalil's did more to motivate everyone else than anything Zeni did.

Sang trained beside both of them. He found it difficult to foresee any occasion when he would need to use the skills, for his role in the venture to retrieve Bellona's friends was defined and passive. However, he could not eliminate the possibility altogether. There were too many quantum unknowns. So, he trained and was pleased at the progress he made.

Zeni looked up as Sang burst into the gathering room, startled.

Sang breathed heavily. "There is news," he told the three. "It is...dire." He looked at Zeni. "Leave us, please."

Zeni scowled and looked at Bellona. Bellona jerked her head toward the door, making Zeni's mouth drop open. She got stiffly to her feet and slid past Sang with another heavy glare.

He ignored it and sat where Zeni had been sitting, in the low chair that was difficult to rise from without scrambling. He sat on the edge and realized he had threaded his hands together and was working them. He put the palms on his knees and made them stay still.

"Verified reports have come in from multiple sources," he told Bellona and Khalil. "The city state of Shavistran and everything in local airspace above it was destroyed by a single strike from an unknown attacker."

Khalil dropped his head into his hands and bent over his knees. The sound that emerged from him was wordless and pain-filled.

Bellona rested her hand on his shoulder and looked at Sang. "Benjamin Arany was there?" she asked.

Sang nodded. "Shavistran was one of the conjectured locations of Arany's secret base." He looked at Khalil, who shuddered. "It is confirmed, now."

Bellona bit her lip. "More of the Bureau's manipulations?" She asked the question softly, as if she didn't want Khalil to hear it.

"A stray satellite outside the blast cone captured the destruction. It was a single source, from high orbit."

Bellona let out an unsteady breath. "Then the rumors about the Karassian's city-killer weapon are true."

"The senior Republic families have all condemned Karassia," Sang said. "Including your father, in uncharacteristically emotional terms."

Bellona's jaw flexed.

"The Homogeny Council of Independence has denied the attack." Sang grimaced. "They say the weapon was stolen."

"Stolen?" Bellona looked startled.

Khalil sat up and wiped his face. "Do you believe them?" he asked Sang. His voice was strained.

"I haven't extrapolated yet. The facts are still assembling."

"Guess, then," Khalil insisted.

"It would seem unlikely that a weapon they have been developing for years, if the rumors are true, would be in a location so insecure that someone could steal it, ship it and use it without Karassia crying foul before this moment."

Khalil nodded and looked at Bellona. "They were involved. Even if their involvement was a matter of turning their backs at the right moment. Yet I know it was more than that. The Homogeny wanted my brother and his fleet destroyed. They were a problem they had no other way to deal with."

"You don't know that for certain," Bellona said quickly.

Khalil leapt to his feet. "They destroyed an entire *world*! Do you know how many people lived in Shavistran? How many *families*?"

"Even if there had been only one family, one building and one life destroyed, it would still be too many," Bellona told him, rising to her feet, too. "Although there were far more than that on Shavistran, I am certain. That is why we cannot assign guilt without being certain. This is such a monstrous act, Khalil. To point at the wrong person and bring upon them the consequences of such an act…it would be just as wrong. We must tread carefully."

Khalil laughed humorlessly. "Who else could it be? The strongest free-state force, the single group who might have the strength and resources to steal such a weapon away from the Karassians was my brother's."

"If that is true, which must be ascertained," Sang said, "then that leaves only Erium, or the Bureau."

Bellona drew in a long, steadying breath. "I find it hard to believe that Erium would do such a thing."

"Now who is abandoning reason?" Khalil said bitterly. He walked from the room, his steps uneven.

Sang watched the door close. "He will reconsider later, when he is calmer," he told Bellona.

"He's right," Bellona said, also studying the closed door. "I don't know for certain that Erium is not involved. I would just prefer it not be. Find out, Sang. Put every resource on it. We need the truth. All three of us have much riding on the answers you find."

Sang considered the request dispassionately. "I have no personal stake in it," he pointed out.

"Erium made you," Bellona pointed out.

"Erium grew my body. The Bureau developed my awareness. Anything in addition to that is mine alone."

"I'm glad you have the comfort of believing that," Bellona told him. "May it serve you well."

#

Khalil found equilibrium of a sort. He became convinced that the murder of his brother and his brother's people were evidence that Bellona was the destined leader of free people everywhere. His conviction seemed to comfort him.

"It must be you," he told Bellona. "You are the only one left with an outsider's perspective."

"I am Eriuman," Bellona replied. "How does that make me an outsider?"

"You were *born* Eriuman. Then you were Karassian for ten years. Now, even Erium does not want you."

Bellona shook her head and refrained from responding.

She instead turned her attention to the preparations for the raid. "Now is the perfect time," she insisted. "The known worlds are reeling. The Homogeny is focused upon everyone else, determined to deflect any and all accusations."

They immersed themselves in the work of preparations. Sang also spent his spare energy compiling facts about the death of Shavistran as they reached him, slotting them into the slowly emerging picture. There was not yet enough information to see any patterns, although the talk, the accusations, the paranoia and speculation were overwhelming in volume.

On the eve of the raid, Khalil sat in his favorite chair, his hands linked together loosely, his head down. "Have you thought of what you will do once you have freed your people?" he asked Bellona.

"I told you. No. One step at a time."

"You have yet to avenge Max's death," Khalil pointed out.

"How do I do that?" Bellona asked reasonably. "The Bureau is faceless and hidden. They have no homeworld to shoot at. Their tentacles reach across the known worlds. They are everywhere. There is no head to cut off." She gave him a small smile. "I could kill you right now. You are Bureau —"

"*Was.*"

"Do they really let go so easily?" she asked gently.

"*I* have let go. It wasn't easy, but it was done."

"Even if you were still theirs, heart and soul, killing you would achieve nothing. Not even vengeance would be satis-

239

fied, for vengeance demands hurt and pain. It is impossible to hurt the Bureau. No one, not even you, knows how to make them feel pain or regret."

"Or do you?" Sang asked.

"If there was a beating heart to the Bureau I would tear it out with my bare hands and give it to you." Khalil sighed. "Sang has more humanity than they."

"I have a heart, certainly," Sang agreed.

Bellona smiled. "We won't tell anyone, Sang."

Khalil looked down at his hands, flexing them. "So much injustice, from so many places. There is no direction I can look where I will not see it."

Bellona picked up his hand. "Look to Ledan, for now. I am."

His fingers closed over hers.

Sang slid quietly from the room.

The next day, the operation began.

Chapter Eighteen

Lagrange Point Five, Cardenas (Findlay IV), Findlay System, Eriuman Republic

Every planet in Erium had an impound field, usually at one of the lagrange points if the planet had a moon. The Eriuman Navy used the threat of assignment to one of the deadyards as a way of keeping junior officers in line. Lieutenant Hersilia Decilla had the comfort of knowing she was not alone, that on Eriuman planets everywhere, other officers were also staring at motionless junk. The only element that differentiated Hersilia from those others was that her assignment was at least the Cardenas field. It was one of the bigger ones and besides, it was *Cardenas*. The city provided compensation in off-duty periods…or it used to.

The riots and protests over the banishment and disappearance of Bellona Cardenas were increasing. It had become difficult to travel anywhere within the city. Between security checks by the family enforcers and the protesters themselves, it took twice as long to get anywhere. That chewed up off-duty time in a way that was vexing.

Hersilia looked around. There was only one enlisted man on the patrol shuttle with her. Everything else was automated. Yenis was off in some other corner, also sulking, so she took the opportunity to pull up her personal dashboard. There were more entertaining ways to pass the dead shift up here than staring at junk. She needed to figure out where she was going to eat tonight, that wouldn't take most of her off-shift time just getting there from the landing field.

Although she didn't abandon her work altogether. She kept one screen trained on the junk and glanced at it every few minutes.

Yenis noticed first, though. He ran onto the deck, blowing hard. "Didn't you *see* it?" he demanded. "It's right there in front of you!"

Hersilia dismissed her dashboard quickly and pulled up the other feeds.

One of the ships was moving.

She started at it, fascinated. It wasn't simply revolving on its own axis as they all did. It was moving in a solid direction. She pegged one of the dead ships as a measurement base and watched the escapee gradually widen the gap between it and the dead ship. It was definitely moving. It looked as though it was easing its way out of the field.

"Ship shards," Hersilia breathed.

"What do we do?" Yenis demanded, breathless with anticipation. This was the most excitement they'd had since either of them had been assigned here.

"It's the family's yard," Hersilia said. "We have to bring in the enforcers." She woke up the AI and set up a channel.

"This shuttle is faster than anything they've got," Yenis pointed out. "It'll take them time just getting off the surface."

"Their yard, their call," Hersilia repeated. She connected and waited. "Pull up the code for the runaway," she told Yenis. "They'll want it."

"Cardenas Safeguard." The male voice was curt.

"Cardenas, this is *Balbus* at L5. One of your junk ships is escaping."

"Is that so?" Hersilia could hear the man's amusement. "Isn't it your job to keep them all corralled?"

"We watch 'em, that's all. It's your asset, Cardenas. What do you want us to do with it? It'll take you an hour to get here."

"Give us the number of the ship."

Hersilia nodded at Yenis. Yenis sent the code and they both listened to the enforcer's heavy breathing as he processed the code.

"That's the Karassian yacht!" he cried, startling both of them. "Damn!"

"Shall we pursue?" Hersilia asked.

"No! Stay out of it. Damn it all…" The enforcer disconnected.

Hersilia frowned. "Well, that wasn't very friendly."

Yenis sat back. "Let them blow their energy chasing the thing. Look, it's just following an orbital plane. It's not even trying to escape. Some digital screw got loose, I'm guessing. They'll shut it down, tow it back, all done." He got to his feet.

"I'm gonna go…" He made a motion toward the door.

"Have you got a party going in the cargo hold, Yenis?" Hersilia demanded.

Yenis looked irritated and coy at the same time.

"You know what? Never mind. I really do not want to know what you do by yourself down there." Hersilia went back to her dashboard and forgot about Yenis, about the Karassian yacht and the rude enforcer and focused instead on what she would have for dinner.

#

Sang looked up at the roof far overhead. "Cardenas Safeguard have sent a ship after Connie."

"Just one?" Khalil asked, pausing from checking the load meter on the ghostmaker he had selected. Around him, the small team they had assembled on the training floor was doing the same.

"Just the one so far," Sang said. "There are no planet-wide alerts, either. Chatter suggests they believe they have a simple computer failure. The ship they sent after it is a tow barge. They are, however, concerned that it is the Karassian yacht that has wandered off."

"Because it belongs to my immediate family," Bellona said. "They're covering their rears, that is all."

Sang blinked again at her changed appearance. The blonde hair and pale skin was cosmetic only, but it was startling to see Xenia once more.

Bellona was not the only one adjusted to look Karassian. Most of the team wore the blonde hair, pale skin and brown eyes.

"So far, so good," Zeni added, tossing bleached locks back over her shoulder.

"Connie is ready to dive," Sang said. He looked at Bellona, who nodded.

"Make it look good," Khalil said.

Everyone got to their feet, stowed weapons and looked to Bellona. She watched Sang.

"Descending fast," he told her. At the same time, he reached out to the lone satellite overhead and smothered it.

"Move out!" Bellona cried.

#

The yacht settled down neatly between the three great fires that were jumping to life in a triangle around it. There wasn't a lot of room between the yacht's fins and the flames that were climbing up into the crisp night air, so Sang complimented Connie on her neatness.

She preened and opened the doors, welcoming them.

"Be nice," Sang murmured as they hurried up the ramps.

Bellona patted the closest bulkhead as she hurried up to the control deck. "You were *wonderful*!" she crooned.

As soon as the last of the team were aboard, Sang asked Connie to take them up. The trajectory and navigational commands had been calculated days ago. Execution was all that was left to be done.

Connie suggested everyone strap in, then leapt for the upper atmosphere, holding the ascent at a level just beneath maximum inertial tolerances. Everyone moaned and waited it out.

Bellona kept her odd, pale brown gaze on Sang, where he sat in the copilot chair, monitoring.

"Passing the tow barge now," Sang said. "They're a thousand kilometers away. We're well outside their scanner range and with the satellite down, they can't initiate a sweep." He checked the tow barge's position second over second. "Not moving at all," he added. "They're quite likely occupied with watching the fire on the surface and wondering how to pass the news back to the city."

The inertial pressure faded as Connie slowed and adjusted her heading.

Sang did a last check on the *Alyard's* position and confirmed it with Connie. She suggested everyone prepare for the jump. Sang passed the recommendation along.

"Everyone, brace yourselves!" Bellona called.

They jumped.

#

The Karassian Homogeny ship *Alyard* was captained by Sandip. He had been awarded the chair three years before, despite the well-funded interest group who had campaigned against his appointment, who had said he was too young and inexperienced. So far his captaincy had been undistinguished. Sandip knew he needed a coup—a feat that sparkled with daring and courage—to draw attention to his abilities and earn himself a chair on a bigger ship than this little frigate. Only, being stuck out on the Eriuman border when all the action was happening in free space, meant that opportunities to shine bypassed Sandip.

When the security AI drew his attention to the yacht dropping out of null-space right next to them, its medic alert screaming for help, Sandip sighed. Another tourist who had wandered too close to Erium and had their tail feathers singed. They never learned.

"Tell it to hove to," he instructed the AI. "Send the medical team aboard."

The AI stuttered.

"*What?*" he demanded, as the rest of the bridge crew smirked.

The data read out on his screen, where everyone could see it. Sandip got to his feet. "*Xenia?*" he repeated. "That's impossible!"

The yacht floated close enough to start proximity alarms yowling.

The screen changed to a live feed from the control deck of the luxury yacht. Sandip stared at the woman's face. "Xenia," he breathed. Of course, only someone like Xenia would be travelling in a yacht of this caliber.

She smiled. "A member of my crew has radiation burns.

We need an isolation tank and therapy. My ship does not have such extended facilities, although I am sure you would not mind extending the courtesy, would you?"

Sandip hid his sudden excitement. All the executive functions of the ship were crowded onto the top deck. Medical was right next to the bridge. He could surely find some excuse to talk to Xenia herself while she was in medical. Perhaps he could impress her with his helpfulness and skills as a captain... "My medical facility is at your disposal," he told her. He glanced at his exo, who nodded. "The landing bay is cleared and waiting for your arrival."

"That is most pleasing, captain." Her image dissolved.

Sandip turned to his exo. Greeta was busy at her screen. Hally, the senior medic, was speaking swiftly, giving instructions on the preparations necessary to take a radiation victim aboard, including clearing out unnecessary personnel along the passage between the landing bay and the medical unit.

"See to it," Sandip told Greeta when she dismissed the screen.

She nodded and brought up six more screens, connecting simultaneously with her executive directors to coordinate the evacuation of the appropriate passages and junctions. The soft bleep of the radiation caution signal sounded. It would be heard throughout the ship, building louder if any idiot was silly enough to seek out the source of the radiation.

Sandip left Greeta to her preparations and went through to the medical bay. There, the quiet hysteria of a hospital emergency was already underway. Sandip caught Hally's gaze and nodded. He stayed out of the way. Hally wasn't above yelling at him if he interfered with the running of her facility. She was a biocomp and biobot, both. Her right hand was designed for surgery, micro-surgery and more. The implements were interchangeable, although mostly she wore the more natural-looking metal hand. Even that hand could swivel through a full circle, for exceptional flexibility. It always startled Sandip when she rotated it.

"Landed and sealed," Greeta's voice said, issuing from the nearest speaker for his ears in particular. "On their way. Ninety seconds, at most."

Hally didn't look as if she had heard Greeta's announcement, yet the hospital suddenly calmed, as everyone looked toward the door the victim would come through.

The first person to appear at the open doorway was Xenia herself. She wore the military breastplate and boots she favored and a heavy ghostmaker strapped to her hip. Her hair was loose. She wasn't as tall as Sandip had thought her to be.

Then the carrier slipped through the door and the medics and aides surged toward it.

Xenia spotted Sandip and moved toward him. She did not smile, although Sandip couldn't remember her ever smiling, on any of the many reels he had seen of her in action. She had been fighting this war longer than he had been in the Karassian military. The victories she had fought and won! She had a right to be as dour as she wanted to be.

The sled behind her halted as the body in it sat up, throwing the blanket off with one arm, while bringing to bear upon the approaching staff one of the biggest ghostmakers Sandip had ever seen. He wasn't sure how the dark-haired man was holding it up. The man wasn't Karassian, which was puzzling.

Then Xenia reached Sandip and gripped his shoulder at the base of his neck and squeezed.

Instant pain blotted out all Sandip's thoughts, including his massive surprise. He buckled under the weight of the pain, dropping to the floor. He could barely draw breath, it was so intense.

Then it disappeared, except for a warm spot on his shoulder that throbbed. Bliss was relative. He reveled in the absence of the pain for three short seconds. Then Xenia's arm whipped around his throat and hauled him to his feet, choking off his breath. He grew still as the point of a knife stabbed the side of his neck. It was a smaller, sharper pain.

Xenia breathed in his ear. "We're going to walk back to your bridge, where you are going to tell your exo and the other bridge staff that we are going on a little jaunt."

Sandip swallowed. "To where?"

"We'll give you the coordinates when we get out there," said the man sitting on the edge of the sled, which was dipping with the imbalance of weight. He held the giant ghostmaker with a steady grip, watching the medical staff as they backed up against the wall, as far away from him as it was possible to get in the hospital.

All sorts of questions rose in Sandip's mind. He wondered if this was some sort of Eriuman conspiracy, except the man on the sled didn't look Eriuman, nor did the short man next to him, who had freckles. Another woman, very short, with large muscles, was removing anything in the medical trays that might be used as a weapon.

Free staters? What were free staters doing with Xenia? Sandip had heard all the rumors about Xenia, that she had disappeared—and it was true that there had been no recent footage of her victories, lately, which had fueled the rumors. Only, if she *had* defected to Erium, then surely the scream of outrage would have been heard across Karassia, for most people considered Xenia to be the most patriotic and perfect example of a good Karassian…

It was only as they marched Sandip out to the bridge, where the crew turned to gape at the sight of him being held at knifepoint that Sandip recognized this moment would not bring glory to him and change his fortunes for the better. He still wasn't absolutely sure of what was happening. He just knew it would be bad, whatever it was. Xenia was a disruptive force wherever she went.

#

Cardenas (Findlay IV), Findlay System, Eriuman Republic.

Wait interrupted dinner with the news, which was unusual. Reynard apologized to Iulia and went back to the library with Wait to hear all of it properly. Even from in here, he could hear the distant sounds of the riots in the city. The partisans had called for a week of protests on this, the anniversary of Bellona's return to Cardenas. Any protest they held always turned into a riot.

Even in his own mind, Reynard could not use the partisans' full name.

Wait was agitated. "The Karassian yacht that was used to retrieve Bellona from Kachmar has gone missing."

Reynard frowned. "Is there a connection to the protests?" he asked.

Wait consulted their sources. "Not that can be detected at this time. The Safeguard feel it was a malfunction. They tracked the ship to the southern hemisphere, where it fell. The tow barge that went after it reports that what is left of the ship is located on the edges of the Caramella desert, near one of the ghost towns. They located it because it was burning. There was little of it left."

Reynard started. "Abilio? That is the ghost town?"

Wait showed surprise. "Yes."

"Contact Admiral Lucretia Carosa of the Edanii, on the *Severus.* Tell her Bellona is escaping. Do it at once."

Wait's gaze drew blank as they communed with the necessary channels to get the message bullet to Lucretia.

"What is wrong, brother?" Gaubert asked, as he walked into the library. He wiped his mouth with the napkin he had carried from the table. "Iulia and Thora are worried."

"It's nothing. Go back to your dinner," Reynard told him.

"It's nothing that required reaching out to an Admiral from the Edan clan?"

"Lucretia is a steady admiral. She is ideally located to handle this. Thank you, Gaubert, I will return in a minute."

Gaubert settled his hip on the back of one of the visitor chairs. "Handle what?"

Reynard's irritation provoked him into speaking. "Bellona is moving off planet."

"You mean she was here all along?" Gaubert's surprise pushed him to his feet again.

Reynard realized he had said too much. Now he was committed to explaining himself. "I traced her as far as the southern continent," Reynard told his brother. "Now, the yacht she used to escape Kachmar has apparently crashed in the desert there."

"Which you do not believe."

"It might be true," Reynard admitted. "The coincidence is too large to assume it is, though."

Gaubert frowned. "If the Pro-Repatriation Front hears she was on Cardenas all along and has now left, then they will assume that you removed her forcibly. It will fuel their cause."

"I know that!" Reynard snapped. Hearing the name of the partisans spoken so freely made his temper flare. "Why do you think I'm asking the admiral to retrieve her?"

"The Safeguard won't do it?"

"The Safeguard is riddled with partisans," Reynard replied. "They all want Bellona restored to favor."

Gaubert crossed his arms. "Did you ever think it would amount to this? Riots and civil disobedience?"

Reynard breathed hard. "They're weak and afraid. They look at Bellona's failure to reintegrate with the family and fear that they will also be cast from the Republic for something beyond their control. They fail to understand the subtleties."

"What subtleties?" Gaubert asked. "After ten years under the Karassian yoke, she came home and no one liked the way she had changed."

Wait raised their hand, their gaze focused upon Reynard once more. Wait had the Admiral waiting to speak to him, then.

Reynard waved Gaubert away. "You sound like a partisan yourself, little brother. Bellona made her own bed. Go and entertain the women."

Chapter Nineteen

Cardenas (Findlay IV), Findlay System, Eriuman Republic.

The final approach to Cardenas was a long elliptical that kept the *Alyard* in the blind spot over the desert. It was harsh and hot when the frigate settled on the salt pan. Three kilometers away, the smoke from the fires that had guided Connie to the surface was still rising lazily up into the air. There was no moisture here, not even at night, to dampen the fuel and extinguish the fire. It had burned for the days they had been gone and would continue to burn until the fuel was spent.

Zeni's crew were waiting with the trucks and carts loaded with gear standing by. They were jumping up and down and cheering as the ship settled, even though Sang, standing on the bridge, could not hear them over the vast engines winding down.

Bellona looked at the little Karassian captain, Sandip. She was smiling. "Tell me again how the ship can't land inside a gravity well?"

Sandip had been restrained chemically. Below the neck, he could not move. He had sat in the upright chair for the three days it had taken to return to Cardenas, with the doctor hovering over him, monitoring vital signs with the tools on the end of her arm. Sandip had watched Bellona take over his bridge and ship, silently resigned.

Bellona had stayed as Xenia. Most of the bridge crew were dazzled by her, still half-convinced she had some great scheme in mind to enhance the Karassian reputation with a stunning victory that required desperate measures, including piracy. They had obeyed her commands with little hesitation, while Sandip fumed in his chair.

Khalil supervised the piloting of the ship to the correct coordinates himself. He did not trust the navigator, who recognized the coordinates when they were given to him. The navigator had paled and drawn back from his screens.

Khalil pushed him aside. "I'll do it myself," he told Bellona. "I didn't spend all my time on Ben's ships fixing his computers."

Now the ship had settled down on the hard surface and silence dropped over it. The bridge crew looked at Xenia expectantly.

"Doors," Bellona ordered. "All of them open, all ramps extended."

Sang could feel the rush of hot, dry air from the desert. It tightened the flesh on his face. With it came the smell of arid sand.

"Everyone, get off," Bellona ordered.

The Karassian crew looked at her, puzzled. They still thought she was a Karassian champion.

From deeper inside the ship came shouting and running feet. Bellona's team would be rounding up the crew and shepherding them off the ship at gunpoint. As the sounds filtered into the bridge, the Karassians lost their puzzled looks.

More of Bellona's people ran onto the bridge, their guns raised. They motioned to the Karassians, who without exception glared at Bellona before turning and leaving the bridge.

Bellona ignored them. "Is Connie still comfortable?" she asked Sang.

"She is chatting with the ship's primary AI. She convinced it to scan for heat signatures. If anyone is hiding, Connie will find them."

Amilcare, one of the original miners in Abilio who had turned into a capable lieutenant, snapped off an informal salute to Bellona. "The water is offloaded. All the vehicles are disabled, although if the Karassians have two neurons to rub together, they'll figure out how to start them again."

"We want them isolated for a while, not dead," Bellona said approvingly. "Everyone!" she said, raising her voice. "Quarter the ship, check for lingerers and toss them."

The teams had been practicing on the replica frigate for weeks, so there was no hesitation about where to go and what small spaces to check. There was a flurry of activity that gradually eased as everyone took up their assigned positions, replacing the essential flight roles of the Karassian crew. Khalil remained at the navigation table, bent over screens and frowning.

Sang counted noses, checked stations, then asked Connie to close the doors, seal and check.

Five minutes later, the *Alyard* rose up into the air, leaving the subdued and angry Karassians on the surface, staring up at their ship.

When they reached the outer atmosphere, Wynne, on the externalities station, spoke. "Eriuman cruiser, seven point three thousand kilometers and closing." Wynne swiveled to look at Bellona. "It's the *Severus*."

"My father's last ditch effort to keep me on Cardenas," Bellona said, her voice dry. "As rehearsed, Wynne. Under them and away."

It was a two day jump to Kachmar, traversing both Eriuman and Karassian space. They emerged above the mostly green planet and alarms immediately sounded.

Bellona looked at Sang.

"Connie is talking to them," Sang assured her. He tapped into her conversations and heard the exchange of Karassian credentials. There was a short pause, while the Karassian authorities checked and while Sang's heart hurried.

The alarms cut off.

Sang let out his breath. "They have accepted Connie's identity."

"Until someone is within visual range and sees the *Alyard*, not a little yacht," Amilcare added.

"By the time anyone gets up here, we'll be on the surface," Bellona said. "Remember the dry runs. It's straightforward from here on. Put her down, please, Sang."

Sang congratulated Connie on her successful handshake with the Karassians, then asked her to beach the ship.

#

Ledan Resort, Kachmar Sodality, The Karassian Homogeny.

After months of living in dry heat, Sang found the moist air over the Ledania island thick and smelly. Many of the crew were waving their hands in front of their noses in reaction to the smells of decay and mold that the swampy land exuded, as they spread out across the island.

Their landing had been noted. It would have been impossible to land a frigate-sized ship and not be noticed, so Sang did not worry about the klaxons blaring a kilometer away, where the compound started. He did run, though, as did everyone else. As he ran to keep up with the team, he and Connie sweet-talked the AIs controlling the compound security and feeds.

"There is a small chance the two of you will be able to convince the AIs to shut down everything and let us in," Bellona had said during planning sessions. "We won't count on it working, but it will simplify matters if it does."

By the time Sang could properly see the end of the swamp and the fused earth of the compound, Connie had convinced the AIs that the klaxons were unnecessary, that their beloved Xenia was returning home, that was all.

As Xenia was a part of their archives, the AIs were confused and consulted with trusted humans, who were also confused. By now, their lenses would have spotted the approaching team. Bellona made no attempt to hide, so they could see it was Xenia heading toward them.

When Xenia had first escaped, the Homogeny had suppressed the news. It would have been too shameful to admit that the champion of the people had been detained against her will in the first place and that she had escaped her captors in the second. Better to pretend she was simply unavailable and taking a long-earned rest from her endeavors.

Connie had told Sang all about the legends of Xenia when they had first chatted. Bellona had woven the deception into her attack plans.

The confused security crews tried to consult with more senior personnel and while they did not drop all security defenses, they did turn off the audible alarms, just in case they really were making a massive mistake.

By the time they got the attention of senior managers, it was too late. Bellona's crew had reached the hardpan. They sprinted, using the pause that doubt and uncertainty had created.

When the automatic defense systems kicked into gear, the crew was already too close to the compound walls for the systems to fire. With screams and yells designed to further confuse and alarm the watchers, the team tossed self-guiding grapnels and climbed the walls with the fiber ladders the grapnels extended once they had settled themselves.

Sang threw himself over the wall and dropped into an unadorned service area. There were doors along the corridor and he pointed to them.

The team split up. This, too, had been planned and rehearsed for weeks. They forced open the doors and stepped into the illusion that was Ledan, with its tropical atmosphere and bright sun, lapping waters and the flutter and coo of birds in trees.

Several of the team paused to look around, blinking in astonishment. Sang noted who was distracted and slapped the nearest on the shoulder, jerking him back to focus.

The little lagoon was just ahead and there were Karassians in the resort uniform trying to round up the inmates. The inmates—the apps—were protesting in bewildered tones, for this was a departure from the norm, from the usual placid life of Ledan. They didn't understand, although the emotion inhibitors were stopping them from panicking. Instead, they passively resisted.

Sang saw the tall, metal-enhanced figure of Hayes, over by the little beach, with three Karassian handlers all trying to tug him along, while he dug in his heels, frowning. The others were all known to Sang, too, for he had studied their public appearances. Xenia's recall of names and faces had been accurate.

Bellona's teams were attacking the resort people, pulling them away from the apps and temporarily disabling them.

Then they, too, had to coax the apps into cooperating. Each of the four-man teams carried the same sedative that Sang had used on Bellona, when he and Khalil had freed her. The teams had been instructed to use the sedative if reason did not work. The first line of reason, though, was to point to Bellona-Xenia and explain they were with Xenia.

Several of the apps were stumbling toward the service areas with their four-man teams, still confused and apprehensive, but cooperating.

"Sang. Zeni, Khalil. With me," Bellona called.

Sang beckoned to the remaining teams, turned and followed Bellona into the heart of the compound. The rooms and buildings beyond the lagoon were a rabbit warren that Bellona and Khalil had mapped out as best they could remember. Khalil had accessed areas behind the public rooms the apps had been limited to and knew that the buildings ran deep. All the apps, though, were kept in the front rooms, the ones that looked like vacation getaways.

Bellona led the file of people into the different areas—sleeping quarters, ablutions, dining. In each, the teams would peel off and search each area, looking for more apps. Sang's tally told him that there were five more to be found. So far there had been no apps whose face was unknown to Sang.

In the dining area, they met their first serious resistance. A line of Karassian military in their brown uniforms were standing with ghostmakers raised. The polished stone floor had been cleared of tables and chairs, which were tossed into a corner. They had a clear shot as Bellona and the others filed into the big, open area.

In front of the line of military was a Karassian that Sang knew purely because Bellona had mentioned him once in the past, when recalling her time as Xenia. Because Karassians loved to have their likeness splashed across as many screens as possible, Sang had been able to build dossiers on everyone that Bellona remembered.

This man, Sang knew. His name was Woodrow. From Xenia's hazy, dreamlike recollection of life in Ledan, Sang had determined that Woodrow was one of the administrators and thoroughly unlikeable. Even Xenia had not found his company pleasant, although the apps were incapable of feeling something as strong as dislike.

Woodrow watched Bellona approach, a small smile on his face. "Welcome back, Xenia." His voice was high and hard. His eyes were close-set and deep, although they were the proper light Karassian brown.

Bellona stopped in front of him, ignoring the raised guns, while everyone else spread out next to her, their ghostmakers aimed.

Sang stayed by Bellona's elbow. He carried no gun. That was not his role, today.

"While you delay me here, your apps are being escorted back to my ship," Bellona told him. "You won't be able to stop me from leaving. We have disabled your defense shield."

"Did you find that easy to do, by chance?" Woodrow asked.

Bellona's gaze flickered toward Sang.

Sang checked with Connie, who chattered happily about her accomplishments.

He nodded at Bellona.

Bellona looked back at the little man. "You were expecting me, Woodrow?"

"How nice. You remember me." Woodrow smiled broadly, showing small teeth. "We remember you, of course. *Everyone* remembers you, including those you are absconding with while we speak. It astonished everyone here to realize that the apps were retaining longer term memories. All of them focused upon Xenia and her absence. It upset the program. Some of them couldn't be sequenced for missions because of their stronger recall. We have had to be inventive to get around the limitations your departure introduced."

"Sorry about that," Bellona said airily.

"Of course, all that damage would instantly be neutralized, if you stayed."

Khalil laughed.

Bellona smiled, too, but Sang could see she was troubled. "You must be quite mad if you think I would stay here and knowingly let myself be used and manipulated, the way you used Xenia," she said.

"You could be their leader," Woodrow said, as if she had not spoken at all. "You have their trust and they would follow you wherever you led them."

"You mean, fight for Karassia?" Bellona did laugh this time.

"Erium doesn't want you," Woodrow pointed out. "You know that, or you would not have come here in search of your true friends."

"I want to get them *out* of Ledan," Bellona replied. "I want them removed from your filthy programming."

"He's stalling," Khalil said softly. "Playing for time."

Woodrow glanced at him. "Your Bureau pet's perceptions are as distorted as yours, Bellona. May I call you that? He wants to believe the Bureau values you as much as we do, which gives him a reason to resist them, as he doesn't have the backbone to resist for his own sake. Yet the Bureau don't want you, either. They killed your brother to cripple you, not motivate you."

"Is that why they killed Ben Arany? To disable Khalil, too?" Bellona asked. Her tone said that this was an accepted fact and not her stabbing in the dark.

"Oh, the Bureau didn't kill Arany," Woodrow said dismissively. "Your father did that."

Bellona just barely hid her gasp. Sang held still, his heart pounding, as he tried to juggle the odds, to determine if it could possibly be true.

Khalil gave a choking sound. The muzzle of his gun lowered.

"He's manipulating you," Sang whispered to Bellona.

She didn't look at him. Her grip on the ghostmaker tightened, making her knuckles whiten. "Why would my father do that?" she demanded of Woodrow. Her voice was hoarse.

Woodrow's smile was bright. "I might have implied that Arany killed your brother Max."

Sang's thoughts froze. It was shock, as he experienced it. Then the human reaction set in. Adrenaline spiked, making him shake. Thought came back on-line, yet it was compromised. Stunted. If he was reacting this way, then Bellona had to be suffering, too.

Bellona smiled. "Khalil is right. You're stalling. You think the Karassian military will swoop in to save you. They won't, Woodrow. They think one of their frigates is already taking care of the situation. They can see it from their nice warm bridge seats and the frigate's AI is telling them exactly what they want to hear."

Woodrow showed the first sign of doubt. His mouth worked as he grappled with it. "You're lying," he said, finally.

Bellona lowered the gun. "Your guards won't shoot us. They can't. If the other apps see the guards shooting at Xenia, they will rebel and you'll never get them back. So we're going to walk out of here and you're going to let us."

Woodrow's whole face writhed with fury. "Your father wanted vengeance. He said it, right in front of me! What sort of people are the Eriumans, to kill a whole planet?"

Bellona gestured to everyone. Sang backed up as she had

commanded. The others followed suit.

"The Karassians gave Erium the weapon and stood back and watched," Bellona told Woodrow as she turned to follow. "What does that make you?"

"There is nowhere for you to go!" Woodrow shouted back. "No one wants you!"

"My friends do!" Bellona cried.

It acted as a signal. All of them turned and ran.

Chapter Twenty

Ledan Resort, Kachmar Sodality, The Karassian Homogeny.

Sang and Connie worked with the frigate's AI to relay information to the military ships hovering in the upper atmosphere over Ledania. The answers and data they supplied sowed confusion. The feeds they looped and manipulated made the Karassians doubt anything they learned that contradicted the fake images they saw of a peaceful compound. Karassians were too used to absorbing facts about their world via screens.

While Sang misdirected, Bellona and the teams led or carried the apps to the frigate. Hayes consented to walking there by himself, which relieved his four-man team, who had not relished the idea of having to carry him if he did not cooperate. Hayes had gazed around the island and up at the sky with placid curiosity. On board, he settled into the crash couch without questions, watching everything that happened around him, as the other teams settled their own assigned apps.

On the bridge, Bellona discarded the hair and makeup that made her Xenia and stood with her arms crossed. Something was happening, Sang realized, as he entered the bridge himself. He recognized her simmering impatience and eased over to the navigation table, where Khalil stood, the focus of her attention.

"I'm not saying we can't go back," Khalil said. "I'm saying we shouldn't go back *now*. We need time to adjust. We need distance."

"*You* might need it," Bellona replied. "I have things to do."

Khalil leaned on the table and took a deep breath, calming himself. "The *Severus* swooping in when we lifted off says he knew where you were all along. He's had time now. He'll have stirred up an armada. Half the Cardenas fleet will be waiting for you when we return. Do you really want to face your father *now*, Bellona? Do you really want to confront him about Ben?"

Bellona pressed her lips together, making them thin and pale. "Very well," she said flatly. "Take us somewhere. Anywhere. I don't care. I have friends to take care of. I'll be in the hospital." She stalked over to the bulkhead door that separated the bridge from the medical wing and slapped the controls.

Khalil bent over the table, plotting coordinates.

Sang glanced around the bridge. No one spoke, so he did. "Let's get this ship up in the air and ready to jump."

The crew leapt to work.

#

When Khalil gave the navigation AI the new coordinates for the jump, Sang translated them automatically. He moved over to the table. "You're not a fool," he said quietly. "So I must presume your reasons for choosing that place are profound."

Khalil's jaw worked. "Profound? I'm not a good judge of that. I do know that Bellona's life runs more smoothly when she has truth to work with. I'm doing my best to supply it."

Sang shook his head. "You have more courage than I, Khalil. You can tell her where we're going."

However, Bellona did not emerge from the medical wing until Sang had the AI tell her they had arrived at their destination: Shavistran.

Then she curtly ordered Khalil and Sang to the captain's cabin.

#

Bellona had a screen up, showing the scorched and blackened surface of the planet, where the thriving city had once been. Around the edges of the nearly perfect circle of destruction was mockingly green rainforest. At the top of the continent, snow-capped mountains took over. The sea beyond was a deep teal.

The view was live, for a burned-out chunk of fuselage crossed in front of the lens as Sang looked, turning in lazy circles. More debris littered the view, most of it small.

Bellona barely waited for the door to close. "Shavistran?" she demanded of Khalil. "I thought you said we needed breathing space. To regroup."

"I did," Khalil said evenly. "I thought this place would provide some perspective to your ruminations."

"I should return to the bridge…" Sang said softly. There was no need for him to be here. He didn't *want* to be here.

"You don't get to slink out on this," Bellona shot back. "You captained the ship here, Sang. It didn't occur to you even once that I might object?"

Sang scrambled to arrange his thoughts in reaction to the sudden attack. "I…did question the destination," he said carefully.

"He challenged me on it," Khalil said evenly. "He didn't like the idea any more than you do."

Bellona looked at Sang squarely. "Not enough to refuse to take the ship there."

Sang cast about for an answer that would encompass the sum total of his surprise. "I suppose I thought…that more than speaking my doubts was not within my purview."

Bellona shook her head. "A year ago, maybe. You don't have that excuse anymore, Sang. You're no longer a Cardenas asset. You're a free man." She hesitated. "We all are. I believe that is why Khalil brought us here," she finished sourly.

Khalil sighed. "I don't think I thought it through that

clearly." His tone was candid. "I just know you need to see this place for yourself. You need to see the truth."

Bellona turned away from both of them and from the screens, too. "I am not a substitute for your brother, Ari."

"I have never thought of you in that way," Khalil said. "You can be *better* than him. Woodrow was right—you have that potential. I've always known that."

"Yet you want me to take up your brother's cause."

"I want you to accept the cause that is right in front of you." Khalil threw out his hands. "Turn around, Bellona. Look for yourself. You have spent a year avoiding the truth. Now it's time to face it. Erium is no longer your place. The Homogeny never has been. The Bureau tried to force you into it, although you should ignore them and their manipulations and chose for yourself. Make the *right* choice, this time. You have a cargo hold full of the best fighters in the known worlds, trained to within an inch of their lives and they all *love* you. If you help them, the free states will love you, too." He paused, his chest heaving with the passion and energy of his convictions.

Bellona did turn, although she looked at Khalil, not the screens. "The free states are *free*, Khalil. They're independent to the point of phobia. They're not going to rally around some stranger, some Eriuman, who says they should fight for something they already have."

"Only they *don't* have it," Khalil shot back. "Not anymore. The city-killer changes things. It has shifted the balance of power in a way that they can't possibly overcome. Erium and the Homogeny will come after the free states now, annexing, occupying, colonizing as fast as they can. Each of them has the city-killer technology. The only thing left that will give them an edge over the other is how much territory they hold. They will not stop now, not until someone *makes* them stop."

"You want me to make them stop?" Bellona asked. "The two greatest political powers in the known worlds?"

Sang cleared his throat. "In the last twenty years, more than thirty percent of the known and indexed city-states and systems have been taken and are now controlled by Karassia or Erium."

Bellona looked at him. "You think I should do this, Sang?"

"Yes."

"Become the leader the Bureau has been searching for?"

Sang hesitated. "No. Not that."

"Then…?"

Sang paused again. Then he girded himself. "There is nowhere else for you to go, but into the free states. If you do, it means you are declaring yourself independent, free of the expectations of the Republic and your family and most especially of your father. You've just taken the best of your time in Ledan out of Karassia. They owe you nothing more. You have spent a year severing every tie and loyalty you once thought you held, so in your heart, you're already living as a free stater. Freedom comes with responsibilities, though."

"Responsibilities?" Khalil repeated, sounding amused. "Every free stater I know would be appalled at the idea they have any responsibilities or owe anyone anything at all."

"Freedom isn't just an absence of loyalties," Sang replied. "It's an active state that has to be maintained. Entropy will destroy it if it isn't." He shrugged. "Just as I, a free man, should have actively protested about coming here." He glanced at the screen. The ugly black mark was moving over the horizon and its disappearance was pleasing.

"Sang is talking about fighting for freedom, if fighting is needed," Bellona said. "He's right, too." She looked at Khalil. "I'm not agreeing with you," she told him. "I'm not agreeing to anything right now. Yet I would like to see the free states for myself. As Sang said, I have nowhere else to go."

Khalil's smile was warm and bright.

Sang did leave them alone, after that. He was free and he was also discreet.

Chapter Twenty-One

Cardenas (Findlay IV), Findlay System, Eriuman Republic.

Wait did not interrupt dinner this time, yet it was highly agitated, more than Reynard ever remembered from the past. He murmured apologies to Gaubert and Iulia, who were playing off against each other, climbed down from the observation deck over the tallball court and followed Wait back to the library, his heart squeezing.

A screen had been resolved and hung at the back of the room. Bellona was on the screen, watching him enter.

Reynard's steps slowed. "A screen," he said. "How… Karassian of you, daughter."

"I am not your daughter. Not anymore."

She looked different. Living in the desert had changed her. Reynard realized he was ridiculously pleased to see her. "You look well," he said carefully.

"The screen is so I can see your face," Bellona said, as if he had not spoken at all.

"And I can see yours. Perhaps they have their uses, after all."

"Did you do it?" she demanded. "Are you the one who

gave the order for the destruction of Shavistran?"

Shock slithered through him. "Me? You really think I would do such a thing?"

"You have the Navy in the palm of your hand. The Cardenas fleet would jump to do anything you ordered and you met with the Karassians on Antini."

The shock this time spread coldness through him. "How did you find out about Antini?" His lips felt thick and uncooperative.

Bellona nodded. She suddenly looked almost regal. "A whole planet of families, for Max? You make me sick."

"I didn't..." he began weakly. She really thought him capable of such an act? "I refused! I told them I didn't want Arany's location!"

"I don't believe you," Bellona said carefully, annunciating each word. "I would have, when I was a child. I might have, even a year ago, when I first came back to Cardenas. Now, I do not. I know you now, Reynard Cardenas and I am ashamed that you are my father."

"He didn't do it, Bella," said a voice from behind Reynard.

Reynard whirled.

Gaubert stood there, sweaty from the court and red of face. He was looking at Bellona. "Your father wanted vengeance, just not that way. He left. I negotiated with the Karassians, instead."

"You?" Reynard breathed. "You did this? It really was

Erium who killed Arany's people?"

Gaubert nodded. "No one must think they can get away with harming even a single Eriuman. There had to be retribution. I did it for Erium."

Sharp pain bit into Reynard's chest. It ran down his arm, making his fingers curl. "Do you have any idea what you have done?" he whispered.

"I have preserved the status quo," Gaubert said righteously.

"You...*fool!*" Reynard gasped. It was the last full breath he took.

#

Bellona dissolved the screen and swiveled in the chair. Her face was as still as stone. Khalil, sitting in the corner as always, looked just as stunned.

"Sang, destroy that footage," Bellona said. "*Now.*"

Sang reached out to the ship's AI and Connie.

Connie was puzzled. "You can destroy things?" she asked.

The Karassian AI was even more obtuse. Dissemination was calcified into the Karassian culture. It couldn't even grasp the idea of not sharing it as widely as possible.

Sang sighed. "Too late," he breathed.

Khalil scrubbed at his face. "Counter it," he said swiftly. "Make the Karassians look just as bad."

"How?" Bellona demanded.

"You have seventeen victims of the worst Karassian conspiracy ever, right here on the ship, not including yourself and me," Khalil said. "Tell everyone what they did. Hold them accountable and hold Erium accountable for Shavistran."

"Tell the truth?" Bellona said. She smiled. "*That* is something I can do."

#

Site of the former free city Shavistran, Shavistran III. Free space.

Even the surfaces of the fused earth streets had been turned into charcoal, which shattered with each step they took and sent up a fine black powder that trailed away in the small breeze whistling through the ruins of Shavistran.

Sang wasn't sure what hatred was, for he had never felt it, although he did wonder if the sensation he was feeling as he followed Khalil and Bellona along what was left of the Shavistran streets was hatred. It roiled in his guts. The pressure across his chest made it hard to breathe.

Pathetic signs of human occupation were everywhere. The buildings had melted, just as human remains had been incinerated. In odd pockets, though, evidence had been preserved. The base of a drinking glass that had run like candle wax. A spoon. The shining, smooth surface of what had once been a flowerbed, with the flowers encased eternally inside the black glass. The shells of ground vehicles, still in their orderly traffic lanes.

Even the pattern of the streets, laid out in familiar grids like every human city in the known worlds, was enough to make Sang's throat close down tight.

Bellona stopped in the middle of the street and looked up at the sun, letting the light bathe her face. Then she turned on her heels, taking in the city. "Everyone should see this."

"They did. They are," Khalil amended, pointing at the lens floating over her shoulder.

"I mean, they should come here and *feel* it for themselves. It won't make sense until they do."

"It still doesn't make sense," Sang said, his voice hoarse. "Not to me."

"I mean, what we have to do next won't make sense," Bellona corrected.

"What comes next?" Khalil asked.

Bellona dragged her heel through the charcoal. It made a furrow in the black surface. She looked up at the lens and spoke firmly. "Here, but no farther." She shook her head. "We will not permit it."

Did you enjoy this story? How to make a big difference!

Reviews are *powerful*.

Authors like me, without the financial muscle of a sleek New York publisher backing me, can't take advertisements out in the subways and billboards of the world.

On the other hand, New York publishers would *kill* to get what I have: A committed and loyal group of readers.

Honest reviews of my books help bring them to the attention of other readers. If you enjoyed this book I would be grateful if you could spend just a few minutes leaving a review (it can be as short as you like) on the book's page where you bought it.

The next book in the Indigo Reports series.

But Now I See, Book 1.1

A lethal cat and mouse game.

To pay off a long-standing debt, Tatiana Wang, captain of the freeship *Hathaway*, takes aboard a politically high-risk passenger. When the *Hathaway* is caught by the Karassian military's flagship, led by the biocomp captain Yishmeray, "high risk" becomes "deadly."

—

So good! Tracy continues to amaze! This story fills in some details for the other stories in this series. You have to read it.

Get your copy of *But Now I See*:
https://tracycooperposey.com/but-now-i-see/

About the Author

Tracy Cooper-Posey is a #1 Best Selling Author. She writes romantic suspense, historical, paranormal and science fiction romance. She has published over 100 novels since 1999, been nominated for five CAPAs including Favourite Author, and won the Emma Darcy Award.

She turned to indie publishing in 2011. Her indie titles have been nominated four times for Book Of The Year. Tracy won the award in 2012, and a SFR Galaxy Award in 2016 for "Most Intriguing Philosophical/Social Science Questions in Galaxybuilding" She has been a national magazine editor and for a decade she taught romance writing at MacEwan University.

She is addicted to Irish Breakfast tea and chocolate, sometimes taken together. In her spare time she enjoys history, Sherlock Holmes, science fiction and ignoring her treadmill. An Australian Canadian, she lives in Edmonton, Canada with her husband, a former professional wrestler, where she moved in 1996 after meeting him on-line.

Other books by Tracy Cooper-Posey

For reviews, excerpts, and more about each title, visit Tracy's site and click on the cover you are interested in:
https://tracycooperposey.com/books-by-thumbnail/

The Indigo Reports
(Space Opera)
Flying Blind
New Star Rising
But Now I See
Suns Eclipsed
Worlds Beyond

Interspace Origins
(Science Fiction Romance Series)
Faring Soul
Varkan Rise
Cat and Company
Interspace Origins (Boxed Set)

The Endurance
(Science Fiction Romance Series)
5,001
Greyson's Doom
Yesterday's Legacy
Promissory Note
Quiver and Crave

Xenogenesis
Junkyard Heroes
Evangeliya
Skinwalker's Bane

Project Kobra
(Romantic Spy Thrillers)
Hunting The Kobra
Inside Man

Romantic Thrillers Series
Fatal Wild Child
Dead Again
Dead Double
Terror Stash
Thrilling Affair (Boxed Set)

Go-get-'em Women
(Short Romantic Suspense Series)
The Royal Talisman
Delly's Last Night
Vivian's Return
Ningaloo Nights

Scandalous Scions
(Historical Romance Series – Spin off)
Rose of Ebony
Soul of Sin
Valor of Love
Marriage of Lies
Scandalous Scions One
Mask of Nobility
Law of Attraction
Veil of Honor
Season of Denial
Scandalous Scions Two
Rules of Engagement
Degree of Solitude

Ashes of Pride

Once and Future Hearts
(Ancient Historical Romance — Arthurian)
Born of No Man
Dragon Kin
Pendragon Rises
War Duke of Britain
High King of Britain
Battle of Mount Badon
Abduction of Guenivere
Downfall of Cornwall
Vengeance of Arthur
Grace of Lancelot
The Grail and Glory
Camlann

Kiss Across Time Series
(Paranormal Time Travel)
Kiss Across Time
Kiss Across Swords
Time Kissed Moments
Kiss Across Chains
Kiss Across Time Box One
Kiss Across Deserts
Kiss Across Kingdoms
Time and Tyra Again
Kiss Across Seas
Kiss Across Time Box Two
Kiss Across Worlds
Time and Remembrance
Kiss Across Tomorrow
More Time Kissed Moments

Vistaria Has Fallen
Vistaria Has Fallen
Prisoner of War
Hostage Crisis

Freedom Fighters
Casualties of War
V-Day

Scandalous Sirens
(Historical Romance Series)
Forbidden
Dangerous Beauty
Perilous Princess

Blood Knot Series
(Urban Fantasy Paranormal Series)
Blood Knot
Amor Meus
Blood Stone
Blood Unleashed
Blood Drive
Blood Revealed
Blood Ascendant

The Sherlock Holmes Series
(Romantic Suspense/Mystery)
Chronicles of the Lost Years
The Case of the Reluctant Agent
Sherlock Boxed In

Beloved Bloody Time Series
(Paranormal Futuristic Time Travel)
Bannockburn Binding
Wait
Byzantine Heartbreak
Viennese Agreement
Romani Armada
Spartan Resistance
Celtic Crossing
Beloved Bloody Time Series Boxed Set

The Kine Prophecies
(Epic Norse Fantasy Romance)
The Branded Rose Prophecy

The Stonebrood Saga
(Gargoyle Paranormal Series)
Carson's Night
Beauty's Beasts
Harvest of Holidays
Unbearable
Sabrina's Clan
Pay The Ferryman
Hearts of Stone (Boxed Set)

Destiny's Trinities
(Urban Fantasy Romance Series)
Beth's Acceptance
Mia's Return
Sera's Gift
The First Trinity
Cora's Secret
Zoe's Blockade
Octavia's War
The Second Trinity
Terra's Victory
Destiny's Trinities (Boxed Set)

Short Paranormals
Solstice Surrender
Eva's Last Dance
Three Taps, Then….
The Well of Rnomath

Jewels of Tomorrow
(Historical Romantic Suspense)
Diana By The Moon
Heart of Vengeance

Contemporary Romances
Lucifer's Lover
An Inconvenient Lover
The Contemporary Romance Collection (Boxed Set)

Non-Fiction Titles

Reading Order
(Non-Fiction, Reference)
Reading Order Perpetual

55286263R00161

Made in the USA
Middletown, DE
20 July 2019